Dear Oliver

Kathy Yoder

Cover Design: Heather Conkling Graphic Design, Yankton, SD 57078
Interior Design, Loretta Sorensen, Prairie Hearth Publishing, LLC
Edited by Loretta Sorensen, Prairie Hearth Publishing, LLC

ISBN: 979-8-3507-3350-1
Printed in the United States

Published by Stories INK: In The Name of the King

Acknowledgements

I thank those who encouraged me along the way, including my friends Donna Connelly and Jean Bakken with whom I first shared my dream. They prayed for me during this journey and shared words of wisdom.

For my son, Ethan Yoder, who listened while I read this story aloud to him many times. He shared great ideas, insight, encouragement, and love.

To my publisher, Loretta Sorensen, who also walked this journey with me giving me invaluable help and much encouragement. She is now also a close friend.

And especially to my Lord and Savior, Jesus Christ, who gave me the idea in the first place. To Him be the glory.

Preface

This is a story that began with a dream. It was a simple dream, yet one that refused to leave me alone. It wiggled its way into my real life in such a manner that the only way I could truly address it was to write this book.

I believe that God still speaks to us in dreams. I believe this dream is a dream from Him. What it means exactly, only He knows. But my best guess is that He's saying something to us believers. Something like this:

Get ready. Keep the lamps lit. Don't run out of oil. The time is arriving sooner than you think when the bridegroom is coming back. In this time while you wait, there will be dark days. Don't give up hope. Be wise. Keep your lamps lit with the oil of the Word of God. Keep your lamps lit with prayer. Keep your lamps lit by not straying to the left or the right but staying the course. Keep your lamps lit with the Holy Spirit. Be prepared. The bridegroom is coming!

Maybe He'll come before you finish reading this book.

Kathy Yoder

Dear Oliver

PRESENT TIME

Dear Oliver,

As I was thinking about writing to you today, a memory from long ago came for a visit. I was in grade school. As you know, that was many decades ago. At least one lifetime, if not two. Did you know we actually had teeter--totters on the playground at my school? You may not be old enough to remember them. They disappeared from schools years ago. Suddenly, they were deemed dangerous. And I suppose they were. Maybe we didn't know enough to be afraid.

We had two of them on our playground. One was a small one. It was pretty safe. The other one was gigantic. It was intimidating, especially for the younger kids.

The idea behind the teeter-totter (also called a seesaw) is that a long board is balanced in the middle on a center support. There are two seats located at opposite ends of the board. One child straddles one of the seats and grabs onto the handle in front of him. The second child straddles the other seat and grabs onto her handle. As they both do this, the long board is parallel to the ground. Both sets of feet are *firmly planted there.*

Then one person pushes off the ground and goes up into the air while the other one squats down. Her feet are on the ground and so is the seat she's sitting upon.

If all goes well, the two of you teeter and totter smoothly, taking turns being in control. It's such a relaxing activity. Up and down. Up and down. A smooth rhythm. But occasionally if your teeter-totter partner is unkind or a bully, he'll make his seat stay on the ground while you're stuck up in the air. There's nothing you can do but wait with dangling feet until he lets you down again.

That's how our world is now. We are teetering and tottering out of control. Someone is keeping us up in the air, while they have all the control on the ground. I want to get off the teeter-totter, but I can't. I have no control in this world. In fact, it seems as if everyone else around me has control over me. You know it's true. You've been here long enough to see how this place operates. The bullies are in charge.

And yet, I'm not worried at all. I'm not even a little upset because I'm not stuck up in the air all alone. The One who created me is with me. He's the one who's really in control. He's my handle, directing my path. He grounds me when I need to be still. He's my everything.

You'll see. Just wait. Oh, and hang on tight. Don't let go of the handle. It's going to be a bumpy ride.

Love, Alphie

Alphina

PRESENT TIME

"A B C D E F G H I J K L M N O P...." She sings in a childlike, sing-songy voice. Sitting on the floor, she hugs herself as she rhythmically rocks back and forth, her long white hair swaying lyrically with the rhythm. Her bright blue glasses bouncing up and down as she moves. If you don't consider her situation, you might say she's pretty for a woman her age, but you'd never say she's free. Alphina is kept within the confines of four white walls, but she remembers freedom. She wrote about it once long ago.

"Pretty. Pretty. Pretty. The young girls running like horses, with new-born colt legs, long and lean. Flying before they can walk, their Rapunzel manes are caught up in the north wind as their thoughts swirl around the compass, too busy to land in any direction.

"'Will they ever rein in their thoughts, their dreams, their imaginations long enough to join the rest of us grounded here on earth?' older women wonder, slowed by life.

"Mud walkers. That's who we are. Trudging through life like snails in ruts too deep to see level ground again. We're

3

heavy laden with the sludge-ridden mundane: Make a living. Keep the marriage alive. Cook and clean. Worry about the children and the grandchildren.

"We're not like the wild mustangs running on the open range, knowing no boundaries, no worries, no fear. But we know them. We remember. When we're alone and our minds roam free, we remember the long legs and the wind in our hair. We remember the possibilities that seem to never end until, of course, they do. We remember.

"These young girls run until they're captured. Tamed into life as we know it now. And for the most part, they are happy. But when the wind blows out of the north and the season is about to change to winter, we stand outside remembering the days of our youth, when others thought us pretty and life was full of possibilities. We remember the freedom of thought and the places we traveled in our imaginations. We sigh a remembering sigh."

Alphina is wistful as she remembers the circumstances in which she wrote this. She was just beginning to embark on middle age, slowly realizing all the changes that accompany getting older. She knows she'll never be young again. Still mourning the loss of that season, she wishes she would have appreciated it while she lived it. She wishes she'd been more adventurous. Her friends always encouraged her by saying, "Alphina, you can be anyone you want to be. You can go anywhere. You can do anything. You can be a famous writer! You love writing so much. You can travel while you write. You have choices many of us don't."

But she didn't listen. She married young and raised a family. A choice she has never regretted, and yet, she still wonders how life could have been different if she would have lived on the road with the wind deciding her direction. So many stories to write. So many people to meet.

And yet, Alphina wrote. She and words have always been the best of friends. She wrote about ordinary life in unusual ways. People liked her writing. They followed her words. Others often told her she helped them through a rough patch or made them laugh or encouraged them to appreciate the ones they love. She wrote a series on loss, grief and mourning. Eventually it became her book entitled, "The Art of Mosaic Making." It's about picking up the pieces of a life shattered by death and making something beautiful from the brokenness.

But that was long ago in a different time, in a much different society. Middle age is but a distant memory now and so is the longing for youth. Other things have changed. There's no place for writers in this present world. No one quotes lines from her books any longer. Those books, the only children she birthed, were burned long ago.

Stripped of her awards and her prestige, but not her identity, Alphina sings her favorite childhood song as she remembers.

Even though no one understands, it soothes her. It's also her battle cry. Hopefully, her battle cry will one day become marching orders. "A B C D E F G H I J K L M N O P...."

Charlie

PRESENT TIME

Charlie walks past Alphina's room shaking his head sadly. Another one of them. Where do they find them all? She's in room 33. That's significant. It means she's one of the earliest ones, if not the first. Charlie lifts the mop and sloshes it into the bucket of sudsy water as he continues down the long hall. The hall that he thinks to himself will never end.

It reminds him of a hall he saw in a dream long ago. He can't quite recall the specifics, but he remembers a long hallway filled with the most beautiful light. At the time he thought, "I've never seen anything like this on earth." It spoke to him in the most personal way, touching the very core of his being. He recognized someone in the midst of the light, but he can't remember who. If only he could remember a little bit more, he's sure he would receive some important answers. But right now, he can't even remember the questions.

Charlie knows this dream is more than just a dream. It's a message. Even though he can't decipher it, the meaning is still there, waiting patiently for him. He knows there's a door involved. One with wood thicker than your head and iron bolts that are as big as a large man's fists.

Even in the trying to remember, a peace fills Charlie. It only lasts a moment. One very dangerous, life-threatening moment. "Seeking that peace could become habit forming," thinks Charlie. "I turned my back on that peace long ago. Why do I still long for it? I don't deserve it."

Shaking his head sadly, he returns to reality. Dreaming is dangerous. Dreaming is against the law. Better not dream or try to remember one, even from long ago. Especially from long ago when life was simple, and a tree was still a tree. When a wish on a dandelion was whimsical and not analyzed to death, making sure it wasn't threatening the environment. When a boy was still a boy, and a girl was still a girl.

When freedom was a word people used loosely without reverence or understanding. The word, like the state of being, was taken for granted until it simply was no more.

Something tickles the deep waters of Charlie's memories, attempting to float to the surface. Someone once told him that memories float to the surface when we're strong enough to face them.

"I'm not strong at all," thinks Charlie. "I'm very weak. I once knew the One who is strong, but I walked away from Him. Far, far away."

Charlie moves his head from side to side, attempting to shake loose this bottomless sadness like a dog with fleas. It doesn't work. Once again, he pushes his thoughts down under the dark waters where he places everything that's not approved. It's easier that way. He found this out the hard way and still has the many scars to prove it.

The worst scars are not on his body, however, but dwell within his soul. These scars don't heal. They're oozing, open wounds. He's good at hiding them. Every former Hater is an experienced hider. "It's how we survive," he thinks to himself. "But survive for what?" It's a question for which Charlie never receives an answer and most of the time is too afraid to ask.

Sighing a bottomless sigh, he repeats two sentences over and over in his mind: "Don't do anything that's not approved by the authorities. Don't even think it." This is his mantra. It was beaten into him. It's the closest thing he has to a prayer.

"Prayer." The word rolls around in Charlie's mind like a spinning top with no place to land or to pause in stillness. He won't allow it because Charlie is afraid to pray. If he prays, he might get an answer. If he prays, he might be asked to do something. Something dangerous. Something that will get him killed. If Charlie knows nothing else, he knows that he wants to live, so he better not pray.

May

PRESENT TIME

May carefully looks through the boards nailed to the inside of the windows before going outside. She doesn't see anyone or anything. She quietly waits. Listens, barely breathing. Her heart palpitates slightly. May knows her irregular heartbeat is caused from anxiety and not from a real heart condition. All the tests agree. Yet, at times like this, it seems very real.

She breathes deeply, calming herself. She listens carefully. Not only with her ears, but with her heart.

"May, you hear a person's heart cry a mile away." She's heard that so often throughout her entire life. May smiles at the memory.

Abruptly returning to reality, she listens with everything she's got. No sound. Not even a bird tweet or squirrel chuckle.

"Hmmm, guess I haven't seen a squirrel for a long time," she thinks. "Once in a while, I think I hear one, but I know it's just my mind playing tricks on me. Squirrels have been extinct for a few years now."

May never tried it, but when food became scarce, squirrels became a delicacy. Now they are a memory. So many memories. So many times, when life was so predictable and unchanging. She smiles at the thought of the childish words she once spoke.

"Mother, the sameness is going to drive me insane!" (Such drama for one so young.)

"Yes, dear," her mother responded, likely distracted by the many chores she had to do. May still misses her mom after so many years of her passing.

"We are such silly creatures, aren't we Mom?" May says out loud. She clearly recalls her mother's busy hands and strongly senses her loving heart. She once again hears her mother's words, "Yes, dear." Her mom, June, was always patient and respectful with everyone, especially May. She never slowed down. June just kept going and going, quietly and lovingly serving others.

When June's beloved husband, Dan, died June grieved, but kept going. She religiously maintained the same routine of laundry on Mondays and ironing on Tuesdays. On Wednesdays she dusted the whole house and scrubbed the kitchen and bathroom floors. Thursdays were spent vacuuming. On Fridays June made multiple meals and froze them. Saturdays she worked outside, weather permitting. On Sundays June always attended church and spent time in worship.

Somewhere in between all that, June kept a budget, did grocery shopping, and read books. Lots of books. She also volunteered by taking meals to shut ins. She didn't bring only nourishment for their bodies, she also provided nourishment for their souls. June was the best and only friend many of the shut-ins had. June quietly shared her faith when she was asked about the source of her unflappability and joy.

June was also part of her church sewing circle, making quilts that were sent overseas. Many of those quilts ended up on dirt floors, the only barrier between the outside world and the inside dwelling.

One day as June was praying, the image of the beautiful quilts came to her. She saw many bare feet bringing dirt in from the outside and transferring the dirt to the quilts. Instead of feeling discouraged that dirt was staining the beautiful quilts, June smiled. "Lord, we are like the dirt on the bottoms of all those feet. Your work on the cross has cleaned us. Thank you! And thank you for allowing us to clean many feet with our humble quilts. Clean those souls with your love, Lord. Amen."

Through it all, June always had time for her husband, her children, her friends, and her church. She simply loved others well.

A few years after May's dad was gone, June said to May, "You never stop missing the person you love. You just learn to live without them a little bit more each day." May remembers her mom sighing. Then June said, "I look forward to the day that I'll see him again."

Of course, May knew she was referring to heaven.

"I miss you, Mom," May thinks to herself. "I miss you so much. No one can ever take your place." May smiles to herself. "And yes, Mom, I miss the sameness. And I look forward to seeing you, Dad, and Harry again one day, too."

May

PRESENT TIME

For the first time in a long time, May thinks about Gray. She met him a while after Harry died in her job as a Christian counselor.

He was a man in a wheelchair who always wore red. It didn't matter what it was. A sweater, a tank top, sweatpants, a jacket, even blue jeans. They were all red. Gray had the purest white hair that reached down to his waist. Some called him "Santa," but he didn't live a life of good cheer.

Gray believed no one could help him.

When he was asked to see a psychiatrist, he refused. He'd seen May around chatting with others he knew. She was bubbly and chatty, which Gray didn't mind. But it was May's kindness and caring ways that drew Gray in.

He said, "I won't see a psychiatrist, but I'll see May."

Little did May know that first day that she would end up loving Gray like a brother. And that she would gain great respect for him. Gray grew up in a home where he was neglected and introduced to alcohol and drugs at a very young age. He thought it was normal.

"How does he even function in the real world?" May asked herself many times.

The first time Gray walked into the room he said defensively, "I don't believe in God." He'd heard about May's faith. Sitting in his wheelchair, Gray had one hand on his chair and the other hand on the doorknob. He looked like a wild animal ready to bolt.

"That's okay," May said. "If you'll take me as I am, I'll take you as you are."

Surprised, Gray nodded. "Okay. You got a deal, Miss May." That day mutual respect began and grew into friendship.

One day May asked Gray, "Why do you always wear red?"

"You're the first one who's ever asked me that question, Miss May," he said. "I wear red because I've been on fire my whole life. I've always believed that one day I'll just burn up."

"And now?"

"Well, now, Miss May, now, I have something I've never had before. A tiny spark of hope. And I've learned something. Hope doesn't start fires. It puts them out."

"Thank you, Lord. Thank you. This is why I do this," May said to herself.

Time passes. Then one day when May meets with Gray, she has a sense of urgency she cannot ignore. "Gray, I have this overwhelming feeling that I'm supposed to tell you why I believe in God. When this happens to me, I know it's the Holy Spirit nudging me." May pauses and looks at Gray.

"Go on," Gray says.

"It's entirely up to you, of course. I don't want to make you feel uncomfortable. I can tell you this, though. Whenever I've listened to that voice, I've never regretted it. Not even once. And I've been listening to that voice for many years now."

May pauses again.

"Go on," Gray says once more.

"Gray, you decide. Should I tell you what I believe the Holy Spirit wants me to tell you? Or should we just talk like we've

16

done all this time?"

Gray looks directly into her eyes, leans forward in his wheelchair and says, "Tell me, Miss May."

"Gray, I grew up in church, but I didn't really know Jesus. I just went through the motions. I was that kind of Christian. The good on the outside but fake on the inside kind. I thought I could create a good life without help from anyone. I was stubborn and filled with pride. It was all about me. I had an amazing job. People knew me and respected me. I didn't have time for God. Everything was going great. I was on top of the world, and I liked the view from up there. But then I suddenly lost my job through no fault of my own. Not too long after that I lost my parents. Both of them. One right after another. My whole world came crashing down.

"I didn't know who I was any more. I didn't belong to anyone. But then I remembered something from a Sunday School lesson from long ago. The story of the Good Shepherd. He has 100 sheep. One goes missing. He leaves the 99 and searches without stopping until he finds the one lost sheep.

"Then he puts that sheep on his shoulders and carries it home. I was that lost sheep, Gray. Jesus, the Good Shepherd, searched for me. He didn't give up. He found me and He brought me home to Him. I'm eternally grateful. My life has never been the same since that day. It's not always easy, but the day I really gave my heart to the Lord is the day that I knew I'd never be alone again."

May pauses, then she says, "Gray, I know you've had a tough life. Much, much tougher than most people. I know that you also feel alone. Do you want me to pray for you to receive Jesus?"

Gray simply nods his head up and down as a tear trickles down his face. May prays. Afterwards, Gray says, "Miss May, I've never felt so loved as I do right now. Wow. To think that the Lord would want me. Thank you, Miss May. Thank you, Lord!"

17

The next day when May arrives at work, she's shocked to learn that Gray died unexpectedly in the night. She knows she'll miss him but she's so thankful that this one lost sheep found his way home.

May

PRESENT TIME

May laughs a little. Now a seldom heard sound, it seems especially strange coming from her. Like when your ears are plugged and everything sounds like an echo, empty and unreal. There's a sadness in an echo because an echo is never the real thing. An echo is just a faint imitation. Her laugh is like an echo. It imitates the real thing but is far from real.

Sometimes May hears the sound of a twig scratching on the roof. It reminds her of the squirrel gangs that once ran with abandon, chasing one another diagonally up and down tree trunks. It was amazing how sure-footed they were on the rough bark. She used to have many walnut trees. Too many, she always thought.

When the squirrels rolled walnuts across her roof, it sounded like baseballs being thrown; usually when she was trying to sleep. Bam! Bam! Bam! She'd get so mad at the little critters. Now she'd give almost anything to hear that obnoxious sound again to remind her of ordinary days.

That was before. Before the day the garage door opened. But May's not going there right now. She can't. More and more often she starts to do one thing and gets lost in thought, reliving memories that are from long ago. If she didn't know the signs of dementia so well from taking care of her mom, May could almost believe that she herself is in the beginning phases. But May knows the truth. "I don't have anything wrong with my brain. I'm just living among insanity."

She shakes her head and tries to come back to the present time. "I don't have time for mind wandering today," she tells herself. "Today I'm going outside, for just a moment." She first looks through the boards on the windows, seeing nothing out of the ordinary she walks to the back door.

She doesn't immediately open the door. She listens carefully with the intensity of someone on the battlefield. She hears no different or alarming sounds.

She smells. She inhales deeply, quietly. No strange or unusual smells. Of course, what she thinks is unusual used to be odd, but not so much anymore. Her normal dial has turned so far it broke off long ago.

So, without hearing, seeing, or smelling anything unusual, she prays with the intensity and fierce faith of a child. "Lord, tell me if it's okay to open the door. Warn me if it's not."

Nothing. She quietly opens the back door, glancing around before she looks down at the overgrown bush that's claimed the last step as its own. May holds her breath. Her heart beats wildly. Her hands are shaking. Once again, she tries to calm herself. At times like these, the only thing that helps is reciting the 23rd Psalm.

She says the words in her mind. "The LORD is my shepherd. I shall not want. He makes me to lie down in green pastures. He leads me beside the still waters. He restores my soul. He leads me in the paths of righteousness for His name's sake. Yea, though I walk through the valley of the shadow of death, I will fear no evil; for you are with me; your rod and your staff, they comfort me. You prepare a table before me in the presence of my enemies; you anoint my head with oil; my cup runs over. Surely goodness and mercy shall follow me all the days of my life; and I will dwell in the house of the LORD forever."

She feels the Lord's peace come to her once again. And there it is. A folded sheet of paper placed under a rock. Just what she's been waiting, hoping, and praying for. She carefully walks down the broken steps and takes the paper from its hiding place. She climbs back up and enters the house. Shutting the door, she quickly locks it. At least as quickly as one can when there are so many inside locks to turn.

She quietly goes to the middle of the house. No one else is awake. Sitting on the floor, she makes herself as small as possible. A crack of light breaks through the boards and she's able to read one line at a time. But she doesn't read. She holds the letter. Caresses it. Smells it. Cradles it in her arms like the baby she never had.

"Lord, thank you for this letter. I know it comes from you. Protect the one who wrote it and the one who delivered it. Keep my brothers and sisters safe in these crazy, topsy turvy times. I love you, Lord. I praise you. Amen."

She opens her eyes and begins to read. As she reads, she knows she can make it through another minute. Another hour. Another day. A peace comes over her warming her from the inside out and she feels safe again.

Sighing as if she's releasing pent-up tension, May remembers the first letter she ever received. She pulls it out from her secret place and rereads it. Smelling it first is part of her ritual. There's a faint antiseptic scent. Somehow, the smell comforts her.

She barely finishes reading when she hears the others starting to rise. They've learned to be carefully quiet, but she hears everything. It's a gift she believes is from God Himself. She can tell the difference between trees scratching on the old shed with the leaky roof and the haunting sound of the rusty windmill beckoning on the wind. It reminds her of a whale calling out in the vast ocean. All alone and infinitely lonely, the huge mammal waits in vain for another to answer. Even surrounded by others, sometimes she feels like that forgotten whale.

Footsteps are close. May hides the original letter and saves the newest one for later. Her housemates will delight in knowing that a new letter has arrived. Better savor it and save it for a time when the others need a little pick-me-up.

May remembers when she spotted the first letter. It was outside the house, sticking out from under an old rock down in front to the left of the broken steps, overgrown with trumpet vine and other weeds. That day she was reading the Bible when she came to the verse in Isaiah 43:19. "See, I am doing a new thing. Now it springs up; do you not perceive it? I am making a way in the wilderness and streams in the wasteland."

"Oh, Lord," May prays. "We are in the wilderness right now. In exile from the enemy. We need you to do a new thing. We need hope and encouragement right now. We need your streams in the wasteland of our lives. Our hope is in you, dear Lord, but something tangible would help us all."

Not a minute after May prays, she receives a new thought. "Go outside and look down." Go outside and look down? Many people would dismiss this as a random thought. But May knows through her own life experience that this is the small, still voice of God. She must listen to it and obey.

So, she does just that. She goes outside. She looks down and sees a piece of paper placed under a rock. She might have easily missed seeing it, but the paper shines with an unearthly glow. May chuckles to herself. "Yes, Lord, I see it. Thanks for pointing it out."

This first letter came at just the perfect time. After May read it, she excitedly called her housemates together.

"Hurry, everyone in the living room! I have a wonderful surprise for you!"

"What is it, dear?" Pearl asks in her kind way. "Don't keep us waiting too long. It's not like we have all day!" Everyone laughs at Pearl's humor. It always lightens the mood.

"During my morning devotions, the Lord directed me to go outside today, and I found a wonderful surprise waiting for me. For all of us. Don't be alarmed. I believe the Lord is behind this. It's a letter!" She waves it around so everyone can see it.

"Who's it from?" asks Frank.

"I'm not sure. Someone named Alphie. But the best part is that she's a believer. There are others out there who are in hiding just like us! We are not alone, and the Lord wants us to know it."

"Well, read it!" says Ben. "Read it!" the others chime in. May reads.

Dear Oliver,

I hope you are well. You work so hard. Up and down the halls constantly cleaning. Will those floors ever be clean enough? That's the sad thing about dirt, it always comes back. Kind of like the dirt in this world. Oh, I know. We don't talk about that anymore. But I know that you know all about it. You see, I know your secret. Who you used to be. Before. But I won't mention it here, since that's illegal now.

Certain words get people killed. But I want you to know something. You are not alone. There's me and there are others, too. More than you would dare to believe or dare to hope. And, of course, He's with us all the time.

Do you remember the old story about light? A Light shines in the darkness and the darkness did not understand it or overcome it. We are smack dab in the middle of the darkness, but the Light still shines. When you get lost in the halls and everything seems dark, remember that the Light loves you and is with you. Allow it to warm you and comfort you. Allow it to shine through you. As our favorite book always says: Fear not!

Well, I have to go. Time for lunch. Gosh, I miss peanut butter and jelly sandwiches. Remember them? How the peanut butter got stuck on the roof of your mouth, but the flavor was so strong you could still taste it, all the while the jelly was sweet, coating your mouth getting it ready for the peanut butter. Yum.

I'll write again. I just hope and pray (another forbidden word) that one day you'll figure out these coded messages. I've always heard that you were a code breaker, I'm praying that's true.

Love,
Alphie

As May reads it aloud, the others wipe their tears, including Ray. Molly squeezes her husband's oversized and calloused hand. She looks at him with incredible love. Once again Ray thinks, "How did I ever get so lucky? She's the perfect wife."

Molly says a silent prayer. "Dear Lord, Thank you for my loving husband, Ray. He's such a good man, but he doesn't know you. Please, Lord, bring him to a saving faith in you. Amen."

Alphina

PRESENT TIME

She plunks away on the old contraption. There's a rhythmic music to it, Charlie thinks more than once as he passes Room 33. It was the only thing they let her bring here from her old life. At least that's what Charlie's heard. It's an old typewriter. "More than an antique, it's ancient," thinks Charlie. "At least from the 1940s, maybe earlier."

He'd like to ask her about its history, but he's not allowed to talk to the residents. Still, Charlie is unusually curious, which surprises him because he knows that curiosity can get him killed, so he tries very hard not to be curious. About anything. He's also been trained like a dog to not wonder about anything, but to simply accept what is.

He watches Alphina remove the sheets filled with the typed numbers. They're in odd, meaningless sequences. She places them in a pile. Then she meticulously tapes them all over the walls. For just a moment, Charlie gets the strange feeling that she's placing them in a specific order.

"Harmless," the experts say. "Gives her something to do," they agree. "Alphina thinks it's her job. That's okay. It keeps

25

her away from the others. And it keeps the peace."

The Peacekeepers still roam the halls, but more half-heartedly than before. Since Charlie has been here a long time, he remembers. More like rabid dogs at first, The Peacekeepers thrived on sniffing out Hater behavior. In the past, even smiling too much could get a patient thrown into The Discipline Room, a room that few survive to talk about. And if they do survive, it's a place that's never mentioned again.

"Of course, what is there to smile about in this place? Or anywhere in this world?" Charlie thinks to himself.

When he was first assigned to work here, Charlie had an encounter with The Peacekeeper, Brandon. It comes back to Charlie as if it's happening right now.

Charlie's mopping the floor, as usual. Brandon looks him over and sizes him up just like a junkyard dog inspecting another dog that shows up in his territory.

"Hey, Charlie." Charlie ignores him and keeps working.

"I'm talking to you, Hater! Look at me." Charlie stops mopping and stands up tall. He looks Brandon in the eye; something Brandon is not expecting. This is Charlie's first mistake, even though his is not a look of defiance or anger, but one of bottomless sadness.

But Brandon, not used to noticing the subtleties of human nature, takes it as a dare. He grabs the mop and shoves it into Charlie's stomach, causing him to bend over, but not fall to the ground. That's his second mistake. Charlie should have fallen over in defeat. Brandon attacks him again and again. This time Charlie falls to the ground with broken ribs.

Another Peacekeeper enters the scene. "Any problems here?" he asks.

"Nope," says Brandon. "Just showing Charlie here the ropes." Brandon laughs at the thought of a rope in the shape of a noose. Charlie learns his lesson; being invisible is the best offense and his only defense.

Now The Peacekeepers barely walk the halls. They spend

more time in the break room flirting with other staff members and telling their war stories of helping to round up the Haters. Always playing the role of the hero, their exploits get longer, and their heroism becomes greater as each day passes.

And Brandon? He's now in charge of The Peacekeepers. Before he stops himself, Charlie thinks, "God help us all."

May

PRESENT TIME

The housemates exchange smiles, warm, weary, and hopeful, but no one speaks. They all think of May as the Watchdog of sorts. Maybe the Watchman on the Wall is a more appropriate title. They know if there's danger, she'll alert them. She doesn't see herself as a leader, but May who never wanted to lead, was thrust into that position, and has proven that she's a good leader and an even better Watchman.

They've all learned to watch the Watchman. To notice subtle shifts in her demeanor. Each one is looking for the warning signs that they've been discovered. Not today. Not yet. So far, today is a good day. May is calm. No worry lines, just the usual sadness that she tries so hard to hide from the others.

May is always, without exception, the first one up every morning. Would anyone expect less from a Watchman? They don't have a wall here, but they have overgrown trees that are like a fortress surrounding this seemingly abandoned farmhouse.

Although May doesn't walk on a wall, she's like a wall for

the others who live here. She's their first line of defense from crippling depression, hopelessness, and unbelief. Her strong faith encourages the others. They depend on it. If only they knew how unsure she is. Not unsure about God, of course, but unsure about what will happen to them.

May remembers a Bible verse from Psalm 46. She memorized it long ago when she desperately needed it. "God is our refuge and strength, an ever-present help in trouble." Not for the first time since life as she knows it changed has May said, "Lord, you're everything I need. You're all I need."

May tries to walk in faith without the benefit of foresight. She thinks of "Trust and Obey," one of her favorite hymns from long ago. "Okay, Lord, I'm trusting. I'm obeying," she thinks to herself as she quietly hums the melody.

"When we walk with the Lord in the light of His Word/ What a glory He sheds on our way! While we do His good will, He abides with us still/ And with all who will trust and obey.

"Trust and obey, for there's no other way/ To be happy in Jesus, but to trust and obey."

May is immensely thankful for her Bible. She keeps it close to her at all times, knowing that possessing God's Word now holds a death sentence. But without His Word, she would already be dead. He led her to this place and told her to bring the others. That was before anyone knew about the "corrective re-education" for those professing faith in God. That was before anyone knew about the executions.

"Lord how can this be the world we now live in?" she asks desperately.

May already knows the answer. With shaky hands, she opens her well-worn Bible and reads: "I have told you these things, so that in me you may have peace. In this world you will have trouble. But take heart! I have overcome the world" (John 16:33).

"Oh, Lord, this world is troubled beyond recognition. I'm thankful that you have overcome it. Help me to be strong, not only for myself, but for the others, too. Especially these precious children. Amen."

May is sad when she thinks about the children, but she also knows they are precious to the Lord. She remembers the Bible story in Mark chapter 10 about people bringing the little children to Jesus.

The disciples scolded the parents and thought they were wasting Jesus' time. But this made Jesus angry. He said to the disciples, "'Let the children come to Me. Don't stop them! For the Kingdom of God belongs to those who are like these children. I tell you the truth, anyone who does not receive the Kingdom of God like a child will never enter it.' Then he took the children in his arms and placed his hands on their heads and blessed them."

"Oh, Lord," May prays. "Bless these children and all the children who live in this world today."

Charlie

PRESENT TIME

Every time Charlie walks by Alphina's room she sings the old child's rhyme ABCDEFGHIJKLMNOP... Yet, she talks in numbers. The ABCs are the only non-numbers she speaks. No one can understand.

"Bat shit crazy," as one doctor unprofessionally refers to her. Or just "BSC."

Today is different. As Charlie cleans outside her room, he sees her looking at him. Alphina is really looking at him, not past him. He gets the uneasy feeling that she sees him. Not the maintenance guy, but the person. His real self. The one he carefully hides from everyone, especially himself.

Then she does it again. She speaks in numbers. Looking directly at him, Alphina says, "8, 9, (pause) 3, 8, 1, 18,12, 9, 5."

Oddly, there's a peace on her face. A tranquility Charlie hasn't seen for a long, long time. It reminds him of someone very special. "I wonder if..." he thinks, then stops thinking and shakes his head knowing it's Crazy-Think. And in this world Crazy-Think is dangerous. Deadly, in fact. That's why he has no friends. Not anymore. They're all gone now. Including

33

his beloved wife, Charlene.

Everyone called her Charlie. Charlie and Charlie, also known as "The Charlies" to everyone who knew and loved them. There were many who did. What were the odds that two Charlies would meet and fall in love? What were the odds they'd be perfect for one another, as if God Himself put them together? That's exactly what Charlie's wife always believed. She was the Charlie with the unshakeable faith.

"My Dear Charlie," she said many times. "The good Lord put us together for a purpose. One bigger than we can ever imagine. And when the time is right, we'll know why. In the meantime, I simply get to love you and enjoy our life together. You are forever My Dear Charlie."

Charlie misses his Sweet Charlie, but he tries not to think about her. If he does, he becomes so lost in the maze of sadness that he has a hard time finding his way back out. "She was my best friend," he admits only to himself. He quickly wipes away a tear that's trying to run down his cheek. Charlie has learned to never show emotion. To never show weakness. He simply tries to appear calm and uninvolved in anything and everything, especially thinking.

Charlie's afraid to make new friends. He's lost the ability to know if they're real or just out to add to their collection of Haters. They earn real good money turning them in. It's a fulltime job for some and a sport to so many more. It still amazes Charlie to think about how some of his neighbors and friends changed in an instant from seemingly good people to a pack of hungry wolves out for blood money. Looking at their faces when they caught another one, Charlie knew that some of the hunters also derived a sick pleasure from the pursuit and the capture.

Once, when he was a little boy, Charlie went to an old-time carnival. He fondly remembers the smell of popcorn drenched in butter and the big poufs of pink cotton candy on a stick. He smiles to himself. "Yes, pink cotton candy has a distinct aroma."

He'd never admit it now, but he enjoyed stuffing as much of the pink stuff into his mouth as he could and being amazed at how quickly it dissolved into a sugary sweetness. If only life could do the same thing. A burst of sweetness and then the dissolution of it all.

Charlie loved the bigger than life booming voice of the pitchman. "Step right up! Come and see the bearded lady! But be warned, the wolf man from the outer jungles of West Africa is lurking about! Many have tried, but no one's been able to tame his savage ways! Step right up!"

No one can tame the savage ways of those searching for the Haters. And surprisingly there are those who pay good money to watch.

Charlie also knows that the Hater Hunters get a gruesome satisfaction from knowing that the captured Hater will die an agonizing death if they refuse to denounce their God and become re-educated, like Charlie did.

"Like I did," Charlie says to himself. "I'm so thankful that my Sweet Charlie didn't live to see it. It was on TV and social media. They still make a big production out of the trials. The authorities love showing executions live at prime time. Rarely does a true Hater renounce the faith, but when they do, when I did, people gloat and cheer and throw parties."

Charlie remembers something else his Sweet Charlie once said. "Think of it, Dear Charlie. When someone gives their life to the Lord, they throw a party in heaven! Can you imagine? Oh, what a glorious celebration that must be!"

Charlie's pretty sure no parties are thrown in heaven for people like him. Without thinking, Charlie plops his mop back into the dirty water. He mops the area he just finished mopping. The floor is still dirty. Some dirt doesn't come clean no matter how hard you scrub.

May and Heather

PRESENT TIME

The rest of the house is waking up to another day. One of the women, Heather, sees an odd image in her mind. This two-story dilapidated farmhouse is stretching its arms out toward Nebraska while standing on its tippy toes, yawning. A singing robin chorus gets pulled into the yawn's abyss as if it's really an alien worm hole. "Robins like worms," Heather thinks to herself.

She shakes her head to clear her mind. "Get your head out of the clouds!" She heard these words often when she was growing up and she reminds herself right now, "Get your head out of the clouds!" Of course, that just makes it worse because as Heather thinks of seeing her head in the clouds, she wonders what's really up in the sky so high. Then, always practical, she begins planning what to pack in her bags to take along as she travels there and looks around.

"Goggles in case there are a lot of large birds flying about," she chuckles to herself. "Snacks, of course. We always need food. And some water, unless I can simply drink the rain." Heather imagines the joy of opening her mouth and drinking

37

fresh rainwater.

Then Heather thinks of all the things she won't pack. Not window washing fluid or curtains. Not her beloved books to read, since she'll be experiencing what can be written in books. No postcards to mail to friends. What would she write? "Writing to you from the sky. Wish you were here." That just might get Heather thrown into a locked ward.

Curiosity is one of the driving forces in Heather's personality. She's curious right now. Curious about the people who are her housemates. Each one's so different. Each one is scared, even though they try to hide their fear from each other and especially from themselves.

"I wonder how long we can stay here before we're found," Heather thinks. She knows May feels responsible for each one of them. It was May's idea to leave the city and come here. Well, not her idea alone. The Lord nudged May in this direction, Heather is quite sure of it.

May shared with her one day that the Lord has been nudging her all her life. "I've never once regretted following Him," May told Heather. "It's the right decision. I'm absolutely sure of it. But still, I do wonder how long we can live here undetected."

"Thankfully, we're isolated from any main roads," says Heather. "Weeds grow in wild abandon in the ditches and on the grass. Raspberry bushes and asparagus patches are abundant. We can eat those."

"That's right," says May. "And there's no visible yard. The old windmill looks broken, but it still works. We're isolated from people, except each other."

May and Heather smile at one another. Both are used to living alone. Both understand what a challenge this group living can be for introverts. But the walls of isolation are slowly breaking down between all of them, this makeshift family. It will take time. Hopefully, they have more time.

"No neighbors live nearby," continues May. "That

community is long gone. Gone when the farmland was seized. Part of the government's big food project to feed the world and progress to a global society. I suspect the main purpose has more to do with control than charity. More to do with profit than progress." Heather nods in agreement.

"But most of all," says May. "I'm curious about who leaves the letters. It has to be someone I know. Someone who knows this place, which means that someone knows our secret. It's hopeful and devastating at the same time. Nothing is ever simple anymore."

"You're so right, May, Heather continues. "Nothing is simple anymore. I'm curious, too. I'm curious about how this will all end. May, how bad will it get before the Lord returns? What do you think?"

May smiles. "A Bible verse just popped into my mind. It's from 1 Thessalonians. Do you know it, Heather? It always warms me like a blanket. It soothes me with the Lord's promise."

"Will you tell me what it says?" asks Heather, now more curious than ever.

May recites it from memory. "For the Lord himself will come down from heaven, with a loud command, with the voice of the archangel and with the trumpet call of God, and the dead in Christ will rise first. After that, we who are still alive and are left will be caught up together with them in the clouds to meet the Lord in the air."

Heather smiles. I know that one, too, May. My question is how bad will it get before the Lord comes back for us? And how long will it be?"

"Only God knows," says May. "And I'm so thankful that He's in charge."

Charlie

PRESENT TIME

Charlie makes his rounds. "Round and around and around I go. Where I stop, nobody knows," thinks Charlie. It's his philosophy on life. His life as he's living it right now. Not before in the other world, where he dares not travel, not even in his mind. But in this present existence.

"Life is like a roulette wheel and the odds are stacked against me." It's a cynical view. At least Charlie acknowledges that. "Cynical and depressing," Charlie thinks. Shaking his head like a wet dog, Charlie tells himself sternly, "Stop feeling sorry for yourself, Charlie. Stop it right now!"

He has no conversations with anyone other than himself. It's been that way for quite some time. Listening to Alphina's singing is about the only communication he gets. That's okay with him. If someone speaks to him, it's usually a criticism or a concern. He's learned that it's better to fade into the background than to be noticed.

Charlie's cleaning route takes him in circles. He feels as if his life is a series of circles leading to one place, Dante's Inferno. He sees the sign in his mind: "Abandon hope, all ye who enter here."

Charlie hasn't abandoned all hope. Not yet. This surprises him. He wonders why not. He remembers something his wife, Sweet Charlie, once said to him. "The storm rages the loudest and the hardest and the longest right before the calm comes. We have to learn to outlast the storm so we can live in the peace that comes after it's over.

"Remember when Jesus and the disciples were crossing to the other side of the Sea of Galilee?" Sweet Charlie continues. "Out of nowhere a storm comes up. It's a bad one. The boat is shaking. The water's threatening to overturn the boat. The disciples are frantic, terrified, thinking they're all going to drown. What is Jesus doing? He's sleeping soundly in the back.

"The disciples shake Jesus until he wakes up, saying with great fear and also accusation, 'Don't you care that we're about to drown?'

"What does he do? He calmy stills the water. He tells the wind, "Peace, be still." And it's as still as the dead. Those disciples are in shock. They say to one another, 'Who is this man that even the winds and the waves obey Him?' They don't ask Jesus. Do you know why? There's something else there. It's fear. No longer the fear of drowning, but the fear of the unknown. Who is this man? Who is this man that nature calms at his voice and listens to him? Who is this man who sleeps through a storm and has no fear?

"They still don't know. It takes more time until they really know who Jesus is. Later, they are sharing what others says about Jesus' identity. Then Jesus asks a question: 'Who do you say that I am?'

"Peter is the one who says it first, with the help of the Holy Spirit. 'You are the Christ, The Son of the Living God.' We know that's right because we know who Jesus is."

She smiles at her Charlie and says, "True peace only comes from the Lord, Dear Charlie. He's the One who's the Storm

Calmer, the Miracle Worker, the Doubt Tamer, and the Peace Giver. Never forget that Dear Charlie. Never forget. And even if there comes a day when you do forget, then remember. Remember the truth. Remember who Jesus is. He's the only one who can help. And He will help, just ask Him.

"Then, my dear husband, forgive yourself and charge forward knowing that Jesus is on your side!"

May

PRESENT TIME

"Who knew that I, a lonely widow, would have this many people living with me?" May, still always the first one up, chases her sleepiness away. She smiles to herself. Some things never change. Since she was a small child, she's loved the early morning. The day is not quite awake, but stretching and yawning, trying to wake up. The day's fingers stretch out and touch the sun. Pretty pastel colors sweep across the sky as morning's fingers tickle the sun awake. Slowly. Very slowly the sun awakens, like the family now living with her.

All twelve of them scattered throughout the big four-square white house, which is boarded for protection and a bit of disguise. If the house looks abandoned, it's less likely to be noticed. No one will come in the middle of the night to question the inhabitants. No one will check their allegiance. No one will look for the identification mark on their right hands that none of them took.

No one will beat the truth out of them in the name of Justice, the presiding religion in what once was called the United States of America. "Justice in this country is a joke," thinks May as she chuckles a humorless chuckle.

"Only God knows what true justice is. Since so many deny God, they aren't asking Him," May thinks to herself. "And truth, well truth is…"

"You look deep in thought, May," says Frank. It's taken him time to open up to her. "What are you thinking about?"

May smiles. "I was thinking about truth. What is it?"

"Well, there are many truths now in this country. It depends on who you believe. Who you're forced to believe. But thankfully, you and I know the truth and His name is Jesus. He is the way, the truth, and the life!"

"You're so right, Frank. God is truth and He never changes. But we should have fought harder to keep the truth alive in this country," says May. "I always thought that even though life was changing, it would never get as bad as it is now. This sounds crazy, but I never thought it would affect us. I think that's why I didn't spend much time thinking about it or even worrying."

"I know," agrees Frank. "I never dreamed it would be against the law to believe in God. I never imagined that family members would turn in their own for simply being a Christian. Or that it would become a capital offense to wear a cross or that you could die for owning a Bible."

"Why didn't our pastors warn us about this?" asks May. "Didn't they know? Were they as clueless as the rest of us? The Bible warns us about this time, why didn't they?"

"Maybe they were just trying to keep us happy. We shouldn't be surprised by all this, May. Jesus told us there would be times like this. When the hearts of people would grow cold. We just never imagined it would happen in our lifetime. We were foolish in our complacency."

May nods and reads from the Bible: "Then you will be arrested, persecuted, and killed. You will be hated all over the world because you are my followers. And many will turn away from me and betray and hate each other. And many false prophets will appear and will deceive many people. Sin will be rampant everywhere, and the love of many will grow cold. But the one who endures to the end will be saved" (Matthew 24:9-13).

Both Frank and May soak in the words. "Isn't it amazing to hear the words of the Bible that we are living out right now, May?"

"It is," says May. "It is. The words haven't changed. They've always been there. But we didn't listen. Frank, why didn't we listen?"

"I don't know," says Frank. "I guess we were like the people in the time of Noah. Just going about our lives as if nothing was ever going to change."

"Frank!" May says suddenly and loudly. "That's what this house is. It's an ark that God is providing for us. And just like in the story of Noah, others wouldn't listen. They refused to believe in God. They only thought of themselves. And I'm sure they made fun of Noah; just like in this country they always make Christians the butt of the joke."

"Can you imagine, May? It had never rained on the earth before. Not even once. No one owned an umbrella because there was no need for one. But here's this old guy building this monstrosity of an ark for 120 years. One hundred and twenty years! You know they laughed at him and thought he was an idiot and probably crazy."

"But what did they think when the animals started coming to the ark?" asks May.

"Like today they either ignored them completely or they made up some wild theory to explain why they were all coming to the ark. I'm sure that all the supposedly smart people had their theories they touted with great authority and others just swallowed their words like they were mother's milk."

"But then the rain came, Frank. They couldn't ignore Noah any longer."

"I'm sure they tried. And remember that by then Noah and

his family were already inside the ark, safely tucked away with all the animals.

"For all the years he was building the ark," continues Frank, "Noah asked the people to repent. He shared his faith. He told them about God, but they wouldn't listen. Neither did their children or their grandchildren."

"To me, that's the saddest part," says May. "That their children and their grandchildren grew up without faith. That makes me want to cry, Frank."

"I know. Me, too. But they had their chance. For years. For generations."

There are a few moments of silence as both Frank and May think of all the people in this country who not only deny the Lord, but they brag about denying Him. They've even made it into a religion. And they think about all the children who have grown up without any examples of faith.

Frank continues, "But just like the people in this country, they refused to listen."

"Here's the part I love, Frank. 'The Lord Himself shut the door.' Wow. That helps me. We don't need to be afraid, Frank, even though at times I am. God is still in control even though everything seems so out of control."

"Sometimes I'm afraid, too, May. But we can't let the others know. They need us to be strong. And you know how we do that."

"By leaning on the Lord. And by letting Him open the doors He wants opened and shut the doors He wants shut."

"The Lord won't let us drown, May."

May and Frank smile at each other, both knowing that they are kindred spirits who have been called to fight the good fight of faith together to the end, whatever that looks like.

Frank

PRESENT TIME

Frank thinks about all he must do today. Getting water from the well is the most important task. Thankfully, the well is well hidden. Still, he's very careful whenever he goes outside. Frank knows about the drones that search out the countryside looking for those in hiding. He also knows, thanks to Ben, that they have a regular routine. They don't alter their path or their timing. Ben watched them for a month, charting their movements.

"Ben sure has an eye for detail," thinks Frank.

Still, Frank knows that one wrong move. One wrong action. One misstep can affect not only himself, but also the others living in this house. He worries about each one, but he especially worries about the children. From the minute he met them, they have taken up much room in his heart.

Jonah, Beth and Erin. One lone boy, an only child, and two sisters. Such good kids. During all that's happened, they have never complained. So unspoiled, they are a delight to have around. They are like a burst of fresh Spring air in the midst of a long, cold winter.

Frank doesn't want to travel there now, but his mind takes a trip to the past. "Now that's a deep well," thinks Frank. "And I almost drowned."

"What are you thinking about, Frank?" asks May as she studies him. This is the first time she's seen this particular expression on his face. Frank looks as if he's sitting in a large pool of loneliness. May tentatively reaches out to him with a lifesaver.

Frank forgot that she was here. He's never talked about it. But in a split second he decides he can not only trust May, but he also wants to tell her.

"I was thinking about a time long ago when I was married to my lovely wife, Isabella. I called her Bella. I know it sounds trite, but it really was love at first sight. For me, not so much for Bella." Frank laughs. "She thought I was way too serious. But after she got to know me, she saw the other side of me. The funny one." Frank smiles at May. "I can be funny." He tries to say it convincingly.

"Okay, Frank," May says smiling. "I'll take your word for it."

"We had one child, our son, Timothy," continues Frank.

"We were a happy and content family. We never took for granted the Lord's many blessings. We prayed and thanked Him daily for our life together. Bella and I made simple plans to grow old together.

"Bella loved to garden. In our retirement years, I planned on helping her plant as many flowers as she wanted. I told her we could tend her vegetable garden together. We'd take long walks at dusk and look for deer and other animals. But Bella drew the line at skunks. She was terrified of them for some reason. I used to tease her about it. She never appreciated that." A sheepish look comes over Frank's face.

"We'd also spend time with our son, Timothy. We hoped that he would one day have a wonderful family of his own. We longed to be grandparents. When the time was right, of course. Bella and I couldn't wait to see what Timothy became

50

in life. He was curious and smart. But even more, he was loving and kind. God gave him great wisdom at such a young age. He could walk between two friends who didn't get along and soon, they were all three lifelong buddies. He had a way of uniting people and mending what was broken in them. He saw the good in others and brought it out. He was an encourager and a leader. Such a great combination."

"That's a rare quality for any age," says May.

Frank nods his head in agreement. "Bella was a wonderful wife and mother. She always put our family first. And she did so with such grace and with great joy. In fact, she humbly put everyone else before herself. But the Lord was always, without doubt, her number one.

"So, Bella and Timothy's actions were no surprise to me the day I received the horrible news." Without realizing it, May keeps bending closer and closer to Frank.

"Another school shooting." May gasps. "At Timothy's school. The school where Bella volunteered in his classroom a few times every week. She was there on that horrible day.

"Somehow the person got in the building, even though the school officials had security measures in place. The person was frightfully angry. No one knows why. Not even his parents, who were clueless about their son's plans.

"The first classroom door he opened was the one Bella and Timothy were in. Without a word or any warning, he started shooting. Without hesitation, Bella dove in front of the teacher, saving her life. My beloved Bella was shot and killed in her place." Frank shakes his head as if the movement will erase the memories and change what happened.

"Then my only child, my precious, kind Timothy, dove in front of his friend, Michael, saving his life. Timothy was shot and killed in his place."

Shocked, May places her hand on top of Frank's.

"It still hurts," continues Frank as he struggles with tears. "I still miss them even though that was so long ago. I have simply learned to live without them a little bit more each day. Knowing that one day I'll see them again, gives me hope."

May remembers her mom's words. She said the same thing to May when Harry died. "You never stop missing the one you love. You just learn to live without them a little bit more each day."

"The teacher whom Bella saved, Miss Jane, went on to become one of the best teachers that school ever had. In fact, she was Teacher of the Year so many times they just started giving her the award without voting." Frank laughs.

"Miss Jane truly lived a good life. She knew that Bella sacrificed herself for her. She never forgot that. She spent a lifetime trying to be worthy of such great love. In fact, from that day on Miss Jane loved everyone without question. Students no one could reach, Miss Jane not only reached them, but she also helped them to soar and become someone truly special in this world.

"Michael survived, too. He eventually became a doctor. That's one more good thing that came out of this horror. Michael said the exact same words to me when I attended his graduation from high school, from college, and from medical school. He told me he would never forget Timothy. He said, 'I will spend the rest of my life helping others. I will try to be one tenth as good as your son.'

"A far as I know," Frank continues, "Michael is still helping others, if he's still alive. I know he's a believer, May. He told me he gave his life to the Lord because he wanted to serve the same God Timothy served all his life. I pray that he's safe, in hiding, that he's somehow still helping others."

"Oh, Frank," May says with tears in her eyes. "There's nothing that I can say. But now that I know, I will pray for you."

"Thanks, May," Franks says as he smiles at her.

And not for the first time, May thinks to herself, "Frank is a good, godly man. I'm glad we're friends." Even as she thinks this a new feeling tries to interrupt her thoughts. It's one she hasn't felt for a very long time. She's not sure what to do with it, so she simply keeps it to herself for now, tucked away safely in her heart.

Dear Oliver

PRESENT TIME

Dear Oliver,
Recently I've been thinking about the children. Where are they? I never see any. I miss them! But I suppose it's a good thing that they're not here with us. But how are they? What has happened to them? Where are they? Are they in hiding with their parents? Are they in re-education schools? I pray for them every day. One day as I was praying, the following words came to me. It practically wrote itself. I call it "Hate Came Robed in Silence."

Hate Came Robed in Silence
Hate came robed in silence one bright and sunny day. He walked up to the children. He said, "Do you want to play? I know a game so very old. It was here before your birth. It takes no time to learn it. It's filled with magic, with mirth."

And so, the children made two lines with a chooser on each side. They battled over who they picked, and the losers left behind. "I won't take her. She's too slow. And he's way too fat. She's not very smart, you know. His voice squeaks like a bat."

Hate stepped in and shook his head. "You're doing it all

wrong. You're acting like weak amateurs. Remember, I am strong!" He taught them with proficiency. His talents so sublime. He had the weak kids crying. "Hey, honesty's not a crime!"

Hate makes them feel like nothing. He steals their hopes and joys. He tramples on their spirits. He turns them into toys. This one's a marionette. Hate holds all the strings. He makes the puppet hurt himself. He makes another scream. Then suddenly Hate saw her. A pretty girl so nice.

He set his sights on wooing her. He figured out her price. "Would you like to be famous? Admired? And adored? Forget the life you've lived so far. Renounce the name of the Lord. I'll take you all around the world. I'll give you what you want. You only have to worship me and assist me with the hunt. I need to find more kids like you – innocent, sweet, divine. You'll help me trap each one of them. Together, we'll make them mine."

She said "Yes!" without a doubt, a thought or even a prayer. She said "Yes!" with her mind, thinking her heart wouldn't care. It was such a long time ago, but I saw her yesterday. She looked happy, young and pretty, but her eyes gave her away. They were empty. Cold. Lifeless. God's love could not be seen. Something had a hold on her. Something horrible and mean. When Hate wasn't looking, she whispered secretly, "Keep the children away from him! Keep the children free!"

"Did you say something my dearest Dear? Did you tell her I'm so nice?" Hate stared at her with eyes as cold as frozen mice. Then he grabbed her arm, roughly yanking her from me. I didn't have the chance to say, "Pray! God will set you free!" I asked the Lord to help her. I cried on her behalf. "Lord, kick the enemy in the head. Don't allow him one more laugh."

But life is not predictable, and it's never been cost-free. I prayed for her, but she chose her own stubborn path to eternity. She didn't ask forgiveness. She stuck to Hate like glue. She'd forgotten about the Lord of Light and His love for me and you. She could have asked the Lord for help, but she didn't even try. Hate kept her bitter and so confused. Eventually, she died.

Hate came robed in silence one bright and sunny day. Because no one was watching, all the children ran away. At first the kids left in their minds, but their bodies stayed behind. Eventually, Hate took all of them. Hate is never kind. By the time the parents noticed it was entirely too late. The children grew into adults spending their lives filled with Hate. So, if Hate comes robed in silence one bright and sunny day, stand up and speak the truth. It makes Hate run away.

Make sure your children know the LORD. Keep them from Hate's dark night. Tell them of God's perfect love. He's the Way, the Truth, and the Light. Hate came robed in silence one bright and sunny day. All the children were praying in church, so Hate ran away.

My dear Oliver, pray for the children.

Love, Alphie

May and Heather

PRESENT TIME
THE DAY THE WORLD CHANGED

It all changed the day the garage door opened. May remembers on this early morning as she waits for the others to wake up. She begins to see it play through her mind, first one scene and then another. At the time, she knew she wasn't the only believer in her small city, True City. A few believers were left, but they were squirreled away in hidden pockets, living under the radar in the middle of what was once called the heartland.

All of May's life it was a place where neighbors were friendly, and people knew one another well. A place where people prided themselves with their century-old farms that were still in the same families.

They found great contentment in a way of life that was now outlawed. Church on Sunday. Prayers at every meal. Hard work and giving thanks to the Creator they loved, even if from a distance.

All that changed for May the day the garage door opened. It changed for everyone.

It was as if she was looking down on herself as she stood

in the garage with her back to the door. She headed for her car, then stopped and pushed the remote-control button on the post near the garage door. She feels the warmth of the sun on her back as the door glides upward. Turning to greet the day, May sees them. People wandering up and down the street like sheep without a shepherd. Lost. Alone. Dazed. The minute she sees them she knows without a doubt that their world, the one in which they all live, has changed forever.

May studies them. Some are walking down the long hill. Some are walking the opposite direction. Others are walking up her driveway.

A voice tells her, "They're looking for food." She doesn't understand. "Why are they coming to me for food?" she says out loud.

Again, May hears a voice. "Because you know the Bread of Life."

May knows she should be afraid, but she isn't. She knows in her spirit that the Lord is with her. Not in some generic, nicey-nice Sunday school sort of way. No. She knows that Jesus Himself is standing right next to her. She can't see Him, but she feels His presence. It warms her from the inside out. Yes, she knows without any doubt that He is here.

She's weak, but He makes her strong. She quickly prays her most prayed prayer after "Thank you, Lord" and "Help me, Lord." She prays, "Lead me, Lord. I will follow."

The ones walking up her driveway stop and look at May. There's a blankness on their faces. "Come with me," May says as she leads the lost people into her house. Not one of them speaks. May doesn't press them. She's used to waiting on people. She's done it all her life. She listens not only when they speak, but especially when they're silent. And she listens with her whole heart.

No wonder she became a counselor. She wanted to help others. To make a real and lasting difference in this world. And she felt a calling from the Lord. That's the real reason she had the courage to take this path.

"Trust in the Lord with all your heart and lean not on your own understanding. In all your ways acknowledge him and he will make your paths straight" (Proverbs 3:5-6).

When she was deciding what to do with her life, May saw this particular Bible verse everywhere she went. She'd turn the corner in church and see it on a bulletin board. She'd open a book she'd been reading for a while. And unexpectedly, she'd find a bookmark she'd never seen before. It had those verses written on it. Eventually, she'd simply laugh when she saw the verses once again.

One day she looked down and saw a painted rock on the ground. You guessed it. The Bible verse was there. "Okay, Lord," May said that day, smiling. "I'll let you be in charge. I'll become a Christian counselor."

It was not an easy path, but it was not a lonely one, either. The Lord was with her every step of the way, just as He promises.

That was a long time ago and it wasn't an easy profession. May often felt very unqualified, even though she had the training and schooling. Many times when she didn't know what to do, she said, "Lord, I'm trusting you. I'm leaning on you. I'm expecting those straight paths."

And guess what? He never disappointed her. He gave her straight paths that sometimes seemed roundabout at best and very crooked at other times. But she always ended up helping someone else. Not on her own merit, she knows. But through the Holy Spirit's guidance.

May makes them coffee in her ancient percolator. It still makes the best coffee. The aroma quickly fills the small kitchen. She brings out cookies. Homemade almond cookies with chocolate chips. Her favorite and judging by the number of hands grabbing the cookies, the others' favorite, too.

They're all ages. Old. Middle aged. Young. Children. She pours milk for the children. Some sit. Some stand. All are in shock. May waits. The drinks revive them. The cookies perk them up. The first one speaks. He's tall. Older, but not elderly. He looks trim, but not a physical laborer. His clothes give him away. He looks like a math teacher, thinks May.

"I saw it on TV. The special report. I was getting ready for work. Then I didn't know what to do. A voice seemed to say, 'Walk.' So, I did. My wife's already at her job. She always goes in before me. She's such a devoted worker. I didn't call her. I didn't wait for her. I just left the house and started walking. Was that wrong of me?"

No one speaks. They don't know the answer.

"That's exactly what happened to me," says an older lady with the most beautiful snowy white hair. "I'm Pearl, by the way." She has a pretty smile not diminished by age. She's wearing pearl earrings with a matching pearl necklace, a pink flowered cotton dress, and a blue cross-stitched apron with two large pockets on the front.

"Nice to meet you, Pearl," May says as her good manners kick in. There's a dusting of white flour on Pearl's face. "She must have been baking," thinks May. "She smells like sugar cookies. My favorite scent."

"I knew I had to get out of my house," continues Pearl. "I live alone. I don't have anyone to consult, except the Lord, of course. And He told me to 'Go!' So, I just kept walking until I heard the sound."

"The sound?" asks May.

"The sound of the garage door opening," says a young man with curly blonde hair and turtle shell rimmed glasses. "We used to call people who looked like him the 'nerdy type,' before such judgmental names were outlawed," thinks May.

"I'm Ben."

"Hi Ben. I'm May." Ben smiles. The others greet Ben, too.

"I'm in finance. I must be really organized, so I always go by my schedule. I never deviate from it. But then when I heard the news I had to go outside. I forgot about going to work. That's never happened before." He smiles an endearing smile.

"So, I'm just walking with no destination in mind. Then I hear your garage door opening. And I hear a voice inside me say, 'This is the place. Go.' So, I went. When I saw you turn around inside your garage, a peace I can't describe came over me." Ben wipes away a tear. "I remember reading about the peace that passes all human understanding in the Bible, but I've never experienced it before."

May smiles. "I know that peace, Ben. It comes from the Lord. I'm so glad you're here." Ben nods.

"I'm Frank," says an older man with greying hair, a small frame and round silver glasses. May sees a simple elegance in him that's hard to describe. Everyone greets him in unison, "Hi, Frank."

Shifting weight off his bad leg, Frank clears his throat. His cane falls to the floor. Ben picks it up and pulls out a chair for him. Frank smiles in gratitude and sits down.

"The Lord was speaking to me. I know it as well as I know my own name. He told me to walk. So, I walked. Walking is a challenge for me," Frank says and smiles. "But today it was as easy as breathing. I walked for quite a while and then I heard your garage door opening. The Lord told me to stop. That's how I ended up in your driveway."

May smiles. "I'm so glad you're here, Frank." Frank gives her a smile filled with kindness, relief, and something else May can't quite decipher.

"So I went," says a young woman with long, brown hair and two cute dimples. One in each cheek. When she smiles the dimples seem to extend the line of her beautiful smile. "I'm Daisy and this is Jonah," Daisy says as she hugs a young boy who looks about eight years old. He glances at everyone. He's wearing the same smile as his mother. He has great big green eyes the color of sea glass, just like his dad.

"Hi Daisy and Jonah," everyone responds. "Daisy looks like a flower that never stops blooming," thinks Pearl as Daisy

63

continues.

"I homeschool Jonah. We watch the news first thing in the morning before he starts his studies and then we discuss current events. My husband's at work. He pastors a church across town. He's been there a long time. He loves his congregation, and they love him. It's a good group of believers. Kind and giving. Always helping others. I called Jim, my husband, and I told him that I felt the Lord was telling me to take Jonah and walk somewhere. It was overwhelming, more than just a little nudge. It was like a giant shove."

Pearl laughs, "When the Lord shoves us, we have no choice but to go the way He wants."

"That's true," says Daisy. "Well, Jim said, 'Then you must go. Don't worry about me. I'm fine.' The Lord's voice was so strong and insistent that as soon as I told Jim that I love him, I grabbed Jonah, and we walked here."

And so, it goes as each person introduces themselves. Each one led by the Lord to this humble house and this unpretentious woman with silver hair and a sparkle in her eyes.

Heather, the shy horticulturist, is dressed entirely in shades of purple and green. Her long dress flows to the ground. Even her hair has subtle shades of both colors. "It's pretty," Ben thinks to himself. The same Ben who's dressed in a three-piece navy suit with matching handkerchief square and shined up leather shoes.

Heather's dress has two big pockets on the front, just like Pearl's apron. Flowers seed packets are stuffed inside. Ben asks her, "Is your favorite plant lavender?"

"How did you know?" she asks, looking surprised.

"Oh, you just seem like a lavender person to me," Ben says in return. He smiles at Heather, who smiles back. As Ben's gaze lingers on Heather, he thinks he can smell lavender in the air. Such a calming, sweet scent.

For just a moment, Heather sees Ben as a flower. She sees him as a yellow daffodil. Friendly and welcoming, Heather is surprised by this vision. She shakes it off.

"It's about the same story with me," says Heather. "I was doing my morning devotions. I turned on the news and saw what was happening. I was in the middle of a sip of coffee when the Lord said to me, "Get up and go!" So, I did. I live a little ways from here. At one point, the Lord said very insistently, 'Walk faster.' So, I started running until I heard a "Stop!" That's how I got here.

"Then the same thing happened. I heard the garage door opening and I just knew that I was supposed to walk up your driveway."

Ray, the reluctant plumber steps forward. His hair is cut in a flattop style. Each hair is in place and stands at attention. "I have no idea why I'm here. It's the wife," he says, pointing to a middle-aged woman named Molly. "She drug me here."

Molly cheerfully nods her curly head in agreement. May notices freckles dancing across her cheeks as she smiles. "I'm Molly," she says with an indescribable joy, even with everything that's unfolding.

"It sounds redundant, but the Lord told me to get walking, so I grabbed the hubs and we walked until He told me to stop. The Lord, not Ray." Molly chuckles. It's a big, hearty sound. "Glad to meet you all." She enthusiastically shakes hands with those around her and hugs the children. Each person immediately likes her, knowing that she is the sister, aunt, mother, grandma, or friend they all wish they had in their lives.

The last three are Kate and her two children. "I'm a homemaker," says Kate. "This is Beth, she's 10, and Erin, she's eight, just like Jonah. My husband, Kevin, is at work, too. He's a teacher. I bet you know him," she says as she looks at the first guy who never said his name. "You teach, too, right? Math? At the Christian school?"

Everyone looks at the first guy. "I'm Charlie," he says. "Yes, I'm a math teacher. I know Kevin Watts who teaches religion.

Is that your husband?"

"Yes, that's him! I tried to reach him when I heard the report on TV, but no one answered the phone. I said a prayer. I didn't know what else to do. The Lord told me to grab the two girls and start walking." The girls offer a slight smile.

"So that's how I ended up here. And I wonder the same thing, Charlie. Was it okay that I came here? Kevin doesn't know where I am. But how can I not listen to the voice of the Lord?"

Her questions go unanswered as everyone is quiet. Each one lost in their own thoughts. Each one considering how they got here, by following the Lord's directions. But where He's leading them, no one knows.

May

THE DAY THE WORLD CHANGED

Finally, May says, "What report?" May lives alone and usually plays Christian music in the morning as she gets ready for work. She finds it a relaxing and worshipful way to start her day.

Each one looks at her incredulously. Daisy speaks. "You don't know? Turn on the TV."

May picks up her remote. "Which channel?"

"Any channel." Several of them speak loudly and in unison.

The TV comes to life. "Here's a recap of last night's and today's events. Congress, with the backing of the President, has drafted and immediately enacted a law that puts an end to prejudice and hatred in this country once and for all.

"'This barbaric behavior will no longer be tolerated,' said the President early this morning as he signed the Anti-Hate Law."

Cameras show the President as he speaks. "We will no longer tolerate antiquated and hateful behavior in this great land of ours. This means that anyone who believes in a supreme being greater than this country will be prosecuted to the fullest extent of the law.

"We will no longer look the other way as Haters indoctrinate their children in their ways and call it freedom of speech. There is no room in our post-modern society for barbaric beliefs that divide people and promote hate. We are intelligent people. And we will think and act in intelligent ways, even if we have to legislate it. Today will go down in history as the day that the great people of this country were set free! This is Liberation Day!"

People standing behind the President break into applause with triumphant shouts of "Freedom! Freedom!"

"All over this great country the Haters' signs and symbols are being taken down," continues the newscaster. "It's about time," he says under his breath. Speaking a little louder, he continues. "These looneys have roamed free for too long."

Everyone hears his words. May herself looks shocked and stunned at the same time. Disbelief walks across her face but May knows without any doubt that what she's hearing is true. The Holy Spirit is confirming it in her spirit.

Another newscaster, a pretty blonde woman dressed in a yellow stylish suit that costs more than the average person earns in a month, vigorously shakes her head in agreement. She continues the newscast. "This just in. News footage shows scenes from across this great land of ours today. Good citizens are taking action. No longer are we allowing the Haters to run our country. This truly is Liberation Day!"

No one speaks as scenes from throughout the country are shown on TV. Crosses are being broken and ripped off churches. It almost looks as if they're being amputated. Pearl thinks to herself, "For just a fraction of a second I'm almost sure I saw blood dripping from the crosses. Oh, Lord, help us."

Rocks are thrown through beautiful stained-glass windows. Beautiful works of art that have survived centuries are now destroyed.

In some large cities, bulldozers are actually pushing down church buildings. People are seen running from the buildings, barely escaping in time as roofs and walls collapse.

The police are shown in full force wearing riot gear. In large numbers, they're standing to the side, their arms crossed across the front of their bodies, silently watching.

As people leave the churches, they are being detained. Unknown to the public, officers who refused to participate in this "liberation" have already been thrown in jail. There were so many, that people were grabbed off the street and "asked" to take the oath to uphold the law. Then they were given uniforms, handcuffs, badges, and loaded guns. Some were even released from jail to serve on the force, their sentences forgiven.

Footage of mobs of people pulling pastors from churches flash across the screen. Crowds threaten violence against men and women who were once respected and held up as model citizens.

A local church is shown. Daisy gasps. Everyone looks at Daisy who's holding Jonah very tightly. Daisy's face suddenly turns white. "That's Jim!" she cries as footage shows a pastor being kicked and beaten as he's taken, or more accurately drug, to a police van.

"No! No!" she cries. "He's a good man! The best. He loves the Lord and follows His teachings. He's not a Hater! He loves people!"

"Stop it!" yells Jonah. "Stop hurting my daddy!"

As Daisy's knees start to wobble, she looks at the TV again. She sees Jim up close. It's as if he's looking right at her. He mouths the words, "Run, Daisy! Run!" Daisy starts to fall. Frank stands up and helps her onto his chair. Jonah sits on the floor next to his mom, hugging her legs.

Every adult in May's kitchen saw what Jim mouthed to Daisy.

"We're transporting them out of here for their own protection," calmly explains a law officer. There's a horrible normalcy to his voice, as if this is nothing out of the ordinary.

"He's following orders from the President himself," says the male news commentator. "He's placing them in protective custody."

What the newscaster doesn't comment on are the signs being nailed to the church doors.

The sounds of the nails being driven into wood with large hammers is unusually loud and equally unnerving. For the Christians being arrested and the ones watching on TV, the sound of the nails hitting the wood transports them back to another time long, long ago to the city of Jerusalem. A wooden sign nailed to the top of a cross reads, "King of the Jews."

Jesus, who's been brutally beaten, is placed on that cross. Nails are driven into his feet and wrists. Although He did nothing wrong, the cross is lifted into the air. And Jesus, who could call down legions of angels to help Him, stays where He is. He surrenders control. It's as if He's being held up in the air by someone sitting on a teeter-totter seat on the ground. And they will not let Him down again until He's dead.

The cameraman switches from this scene to the nearby wooden cross on the church's front lawn. Large nails are sticking out from the wood. Someone has placed a crown of thorns at the top of the cross.

The camera footage goes back to the signs. Some are printed in large block letters: "Pastors Prohibited." Others read: "Closed Forever." And still others: "Trespassers will be prosecuted."

May and the others almost miss the last one. "Turn in Pastors. Turn in Haters. Big reward."

A chill starts at the top of May's head and travels all the way down to her toes. Somehow, she knew that this day would come, but she prayed that she was wrong. All thoughts about going to work are forgotten, which is good since any business with the name "Christian" attached to it is being shut down and the authorities are arresting all the employees "for their own protection."

Live footage of teachers, staff, and children being pulled from the local Christian school is now on the TV. More police are shown in riot gear. "The police are present in case there are any unruly protestors," says the newscaster.

But there are no protestors. The quickest thinkers are already on the move. They realize, contrary to the news coverage, that they are running for their lives. Crowds of people are shouting obscenities as the believers are being placed under the so-called protective custody.

"That's Kevin!" cries Kate as her two daughters cling to her. "That's our daddy! That's our daddy!" cry Beth and Erin.

Kevin is placed in handcuffs. They're not even pretending anymore. Someone from the crowd kicks him. Another person spits on him. The crowd starts yelling, "Haters! Haters! Kill the Haters! Kill them! Kill them all!"

May grabs her Bible off the kitchen table and holds it next to her heart like a lifeline. She prays silently. "Lord, we need your straight paths right now!"

May

THE DAY THE WORLD CHANGED

"This just in," continues the female newscaster. "All Haters are required to go immediately to their county courthouse to register for their own protection. They should bring one suitcase with them filled with medications and other needed items including their birth certificate, driver's license, and passport if they have one. If they do not comply, they will be found and arrested.

"Don't try to run. There's nowhere to go. We know where you live. We've mapped out every household in this great country from the urban cities to the rural areas. If you've ever attended a church, given to a Hater group, or written anything in social media that suggests that you believe in this so-called God, we know all about it. We'll find you. We probably already have.

"Furthermore, after today, all loyal citizens will make their way to the courthouse within the next month and receive a painless loyalty mark with accompanying chip inserted under the palm of their right hand. From now on, no one will be able to buy, sell, or trade without this mark."

The camera shows the President again. Looking appropriately serious and perfectly coiffed as always, he says, "It's the right thing to do. The only thing to do. After next month, if you do not take the loyalty mark you will be in violation of your civil duty. We will assume that you no longer want to be a citizen of this great country. And you will be dealt with as a foreign enemy. Justice will be carried out swiftly for the safety of all our loyal citizens.

"I was elected to serve the people of this great land and I plan on doing just that. No more will we sit idly by as our values, our beliefs, and our morals are compromised for a small, hateful group of antiquated people. We are a united country with united goals and united beliefs.

"Eventually, we expect to become part of a united global society where all men, women, and others will live in peace," he says with religious fervor.

The President is now standing outside. Behind him is a large pile of burning books. The fire is glowing a deep red. In an odd way, the fire outlines the president, making him appear almost satanic.

Men dressed in red riot gear are adding more books to the pile. The President looks at the burning books and says, "All citizens are to surrender their hate books to my special police. You will recognize them because they're dressed entirely in red. I call them 'The Red Coats.'"

The President pauses to smile. Something happens that makes May stop. For just a moment, she doesn't see the President. She sees a demon surrounded by a glowing red fire. May shakes her head, trying to make the horrific image disappear. In a moment, the image is gone.

"Did I imagine that?" May whispers. She catches Pearl's eye. Pearl is looking directly at May. "No, you did not," Pearl says. "I saw it, too. We just saw the face of evil."

"All Bibles and any other propaganda books that are written by Haters," continues the President, "as well as any symbols

74

worn by Haters, are all outlawed as of this very moment. They must be surrendered by the end of the week. If we hear of Haters hording books, or crosses, or those silly fish symbols, you will be dealt with swiftly and justly.

"We are ushering in a new era. A time for peace and love between the people of this great country and the people of the world. Soon, we will embark on a new and promising journey of freedom throughout the globe.

"We will no longer be merely citizens of this country. We are now a global society united for the good of all men, women, and other kind. All borders will immediately be removed. We will no longer live in fear of one another. We will join together to form a utopia here on earth. We will build a better society with our brothers and sisters and others throughout the globe.

"We shall all live in peace and harmony from this day forward. This is indeed Liberation Day. And not just for our country but for the entire world!"

The President speaks with a fervor that can only be compared to the old evangelists from long ago. Although this message is quite different and the Lord is not involved in anything the President says, or thinks, or does.

May is stunned. She can't move or think or speak for a good two minutes at least, although it seems like days.

The rest of the kitchen crew look completely lost, dazed, and shocked. Like May, they don't know what to do or where to go. It's like a movie scene when time completely stops. There's no movement. Everyone and everything are frozen in time. Even clocks are stopped. There's literally no passage of time.

Something in this world so shocking has occurred that even nature stops to pause. No birds are singing. No wind is blowing. No movement of any kind exists inside or outside. Everything and everyone are completely still.

"I wonder," says Pearl. "Has even heaven stopped and paused by what has just happened?" She doesn't expect an answer. She's simply curious, amazed by what has just occurred.

In fact, everyone in May's kitchen is overwhelmed by the magnitude of it all. May realizes it's like in an old sci fi movie she saw long ago when the inmates in the insane asylum took over and ran the place. What was once thought unthinkable became the norm. And once normal people were now deemed completely insane.

As May looks around at the people in her home whom she just met mere moments ago, she feels responsible for them. For each one. With a holy nudge, May knows what she must do. She is being called to take charge. She doesn't see herself as a leader, but she knows that at least in this one moment, the Lord is calling her to act for such a time as this.

May also knows who this group is and who they will become. Only moments ago, they were complete strangers. But now they are a makeshift family formed in a few terrible moments called to live together in secret. They are the remnant the Bible talks about.

"And the dragon was wroth with the woman, and went to make war with the remnant of her seed, which keep the commandments of God, and have the testimony of Jesus Christ" (Revelation 12:17).

"Oh yes," thinks May. "We have the testimony of Jesus Christ. Not only the testimony of what He has done in each one of our lives, but we are also the living testimony of what He will do. If we follow and obey, He will lead us."

May unconsciously begins humming the old hymn, "Trust and Obey."

"When we walk with the Lord in the light of His Word/ What a glory He sheds on our way!/ While we do His good will, He abides with us still/ And with all who will trust and obey."

Some of the others join in singing and humming. Pearl, who has a beautiful voice, takes the lead. And this hymn becomes a promise and a prayer.

May

THE DAY THE WORLD CHANGED

"Well, one thing is for sure," says May. "We're not going to the courthouse. We're not turning ourselves in. We're definitely not taking a loyalty mark. We are loyal to Jesus Christ who is the same yesterday, today, and forever. We are Christ Followers. We are not Haters. We are called to live a life of love, not a life of hate.

"And we have something they don't have. We have the God of Angel Armies on our side." May speaks with a confidence, a strength, and a wisdom that does not come from herself.

"What are we going to do?" asks Daisy, crying as she hugs Jonah tightly.

"We're going to take a little trip to the country," says May. "I know a farmhouse where no one lives. We'll stay there. For now." Everyone nods in agreement because no one knows what else to do.

The TV's still on. Live coverage of the Christian Counseling Center where May works is highlighted. Counselors and clients alike are being led out by gun point and loaded into police vans. One person breaks from the line and runs down the street. Slowly, methodically, he's shot down. He falls to the ground. He's left there. The van drives away. The newscasters aren't speaking. They simply smile at one another. It's a smug smile. One that speaks loudly without words.

May sees it all and knows that she'll never return to this house or the life she once had a mere 10 minutes ago. "Help us, Lord," she prays. "Only you can."

All three children have backpacks. May instructs the others to fill them up with canned goods and other supplies from her pantry. They grab a first aid kit and all the flashlights and batteries they can find. Luckily, May has a big supply of water. They pack everything and anything they can find.

May gathers up her extra Bibles. Ray is watching her. "We'll need these most of all," she says. Ray shrugs, looking doubtful.

"I have a pickup truck and a car. We'll take both. We'll leave soon," says May. "While we still can. Hopefully, they haven't set up roadblocks yet. At least they didn't mention them on TV."

May knows the back roads well. That's the way she'll lead them, with the Lord's help, through the gravel and the mud. The roads should still be clear enough. It hasn't rained for a while.

"I can't go," says Charlie. "I can't go. I must find my wife. She's... she's a pastor. At a church. She's my ... everything. I have to go find my Sweet Charlie." Charlie is visibly shaking.

"It's okay, Charlie," says May soothingly, as if she's comforting a small child. "You go get her and bring her with you to us. I'll tell you the directions. I don't want to draw you a map. It's too dangerous. Can you remember them?"

"Yes, I have the best memory," says Charlie. "A photographic one. I can picture the words as you speak them."

May gives him detailed directions, even telling him which backroads to take and which ones to avoid, depending on the season. May hugs Charlie and whispers, "God be with you! Go get your girl!"

"I will," says Charlie, choking back sobs. "I will."

Charlie

THE DAY THE WORLD CHANGED

Charlie walks as fast as he can back to his own home. He sees his neighbor, Al, standing outside their house. Al's an okay guy. He never wants much to do with church. He keeps to himself but is friendly enough. As Charlie gets close, Al waves him over.

"Come here, ole' buddy," he says.

"That's odd," thinks Charlie. "When did I become his buddy?"

He sees Al's right arm behind his back. Before he can react, Charlie sees the rifle. Instinctively, he begins to turn away, but a voice stops him.

"Charlie," says his Sweet Charlie. Her voice sounds small and scared. "Odd," thinks Charlie. "I've never heard her voice sound like that before."

He looks around for her. Amid unfolding trauma, time can sometimes seem to slow down as the human brain attempts to make logical sense out of the illogical. Everything seems to be moving in very slow motion right now, as if Charlie has all the time in the world.

Then he spots her. He can't understand what he's seeing

with his own eyes. He even rubs them to make sure that what he's seeing is true. He opens his eyes. Nothing has changed. His Sweet Charlie is lying in Al's truck bed. Tied up like a Thanksgiving Day turkey, she's still wearing her clerical collar. "What an odd sight," thinks Charlie. He just might laugh, if he wasn't so confused and scared. He's not even sure what he's afraid of. But somewhere from deep inside the marrow of his bones, fear rises up and envelops him.

Charlie shakes his head, trying to reconcile the scene before him. It just doesn't add up. Why is his Sweet Charlie tied up? What's Al up to? Why does he have his rifle? The one he uses for deer hunting. He's even dressed in camo.

Al laughs. "Hey, good buddy! You're not going to make this hard for me, are you? Get in the truck with your wife now. No funny stuff. I'm aiming right at her head."

Still dazed, Charlie does what he's told. As Al taps Charlie on the head with his rifle, Charlie hears him singing, "Going to get the big reward. Going to get the big reward." There's a joy in his voice that Charlie's never heard before.

Right before he loses consciousness completely, Charlie sees his neighbors watching. They're standing in their yards and near the street. It's almost as if they're standing at attention like we did long ago when the National Anthem was being played.

But then Charlie thinks back to an old photo from an old history book. The kind that's been outlawed for many years. The photo and the history. He sees people watching as the Jews are being led to the trains. And the people, their friends and their neighbors, are smiling horrible smiles.

Over the years, many have said that the Holocaust never happened. That it was made up to make good people look bad. But Charlie remembers a neighborhood kid's grandma from long ago. He saw the numbers tattooed on her arm. She had survived the concentration camps during World War II, but she never forgot. And she made it her personal mission to tell all the children she could about what happened. Not to scare them, but to arm them against the lies, which she believed would come again.

"I'm telling you about these things to inform you and to also warn you," the grandmother said. "This did happen. Don't believe people who tell you that it didn't happen. They're lying. I was there. I lost my entire family. My beloved parents who loved us all so much that they would die for us did just that. They died trying to protect us. My two brothers and three sisters who were all my best friends, each one of them protected me. I was the youngest. They even shared their bread with me even though they were starving.

"Out of my whole family, I alone lived through that hell" she continued. "I don't know why God spared me, but I suspect that one of the reasons is to tell others about what happened.

"Don't let history repeat itself." She trembled as she voiced the warning. "Never forget to thank God for the freedom we have in this country. Satan himself was in charge of that horrific time when Hitler wanted to wipe the Jewish people from the face of the earth. Unthinkable things happen when hate is in control. Never, never, ever forget."

Charlie senses a deep chill as he visualizes what he just saw; his neighbors smiling their horrible smiles. Their smiles and the photos of the Nazi sympathizers' smiles overlap in his mind. He can't tell where his neighbors end, and the others begin. They look the same; horrifically the same.

Charlie shivers and passes out as he hears the old woman's words once more. "Never, never, ever forget."

May

THE DAY THE WORLD CHANGED

Quickly and carefully, May leads the others to the garage; the place where all this started. She makes sure the door is closed. They load up the car and the old red pickup truck, which once belonged to her husband, Harry. She didn't have the heart to sell it when he died. It's been a comforting reminder of him ever since.

Besides, she likes the truck because it's red, Harry's favorite color. Well, his favorite color was red plaid on a flannel shirt, Harry's unspoken uniform. She also likes the truck because it's so easy to drive. Harry liked it because it was practical. Now she's especially thankful that she still has it.

"May, do you have a tarp to put over the truck bed?" asks Ben.

"Don't need one," says May. "It has a built-in cover."

"Great. I see it now." Ben and Ray load the provisions in the truck as the women decide where everyone should sit.

"I really think I should sit up front in the truck," says Pearl. "They'll take one look at me and think, 'Oh, she's a harmless old lady.'" Pearl chuckles at the thought.

"We should put the kids and moms in the truck bed, if

there's room," says Daisy.

"We can put the blankets on the bed," agrees Kate. "That should make it more comfortable, and we can hide under them if we have to."

"Frank, I think you should drive the car and I'll sit up front with you," May says. "We can lead the way. And we can pretend to be a couple, if you don't mind."

"Good idea," says Frank, smiling.

The car leads the truck through chaotic streets. They see neighbors chasing down neighbors like something from a horror film. Police in riot gear are knocking on doors. Many authorities are using battery rams to gain entrance. Some are led to homes by once-trusted neighbors.

May and the others quietly drive out of the city, leaving the noise and mayhem behind. They drive on hilly, winding curves and down into deep, mist-filled valleys. The terrain is as different as the people in the two vehicles.

May leads them on deserted gravel roads for what seems like many miles until they finally reach an unassuming road. There's an old, weather-beaten wooden sign that reads: "Not Maintained." Part of the sign hangs down where the nail rusted away.

"Turn, here," May tells Frank. "Slowly." The pickup follows. The road sports big bumps and deep crevices with fallen shoulders. Driving on the road is similar to driving on an obstacle course, but much more challenging.

"Up ahead," says May.

"Where?" asks Frank as he strains to see.

"That grove of spruce trees."

They arrive with no road in sight. "Between those two trees," says May. "You can make it."

Frank gingerly drives beyond the road with the pickup close behind. He would never attempt this way if May wasn't by his side. Even though he's just met her, he senses he can trust her.

Why can he trust her? Frank has discovered that during times of greatest need, the Lord is always with him.

"During times like this," thinks Frank, "the Lord always brings good people to me. May seems like one of those good people right now. I've learned to lean on Him. He never lets me down. In times of trouble, He's the One to turn to."

Frank is lost in his thoughts about the Lord's presence during some of the hardest moments of his life. "I'm so thankful," he says.

"What?" asks May. Frank forgot for just a moment where he was.

"Oh, nothing. Just thanking the Lord for being with me. With all of us."

"Amen," says May. "Amen."

May

PRESENT TIME

Someone jostles Charlie awake. As he and his wife Sweet Charlie are led into the courthouse, they see many familiar faces. Almost everyone from Pastor Charlie's church is present. Like lost sheep, her people look to her for guidance. She smiles reassuringly at each one, but they want more. With great strength she knows does not come from herself, Pastor Charlie mouths one word to them all: "Pray."

In her ministry she's always told her people not to wait to talk to the Lord until things get bad. "Talk to Him every day so that you know His voice. Then you won't get His voice mixed up with other voices. There are many voices in our culture vying for our attention. 'Be popular! Get rich! Have an easy life! You can have it all. There's nothing after this life. Grab all you can get now!'

"Remember what Jesus said?" asks Pastor Charlie now. 'My sheep know my voice and they follow me.' Don't follow anyone but Jesus. He's the only one who can truly find us when we're lost. He's the only one who can truly set us free."

"We need that freedom right now, Lord," her husband

thinks to himself. How can his Sweet Charlie be so calm? She's a leader, he knows that, but her faith must be deep. Very deep. "Much deeper than mine." The thought barely crosses his mind before fear settles into the very marrow of his bones and begins invading his soul.

His thoughts are interrupted by a large man with a big gun. "Follow me," he says, looking at the Charlies. It's not a request but a demand.

May

THE DAY THE WORLD CHANGED

May directs Frank to an old outbuilding. They park both the truck and car inside. It's hard to get the overhead door open and then closed again. Everything's rusted by age and neglect. An old tractor sits in the corner. It sports cobwebs much older than the children.

"Take these branches and help me wipe out the tracks and our footsteps as we go to the house," says May.

"What house?" asks Frank.

"Just follow me. It's behind those trees."

There's a grove of ancient spruce trees more than 75 feet tall around the outbuildings, They've grown so closely together, they look like a wall. And there's also another grove within that grove. It's just as old and just as tall. Like something out of a fairy tale, there's the hidden, hiding within the hidden.

Tucked inside that inner grove is an old, abandoned farmhouse. May stops when she sees it. Memories flood her mind. Happy memories of her life with her beloved husband, Harry. He's been gone too long. What would he say of all this?

"I know what he'd say," thinks May. "He'd say, 'May Day,

I told you this day was coming. It's in the Good Book.'" May Day was Harry's pet name for her.

"And then he'd say, 'Hold on tight to the Lord. It's going to be a bumpy ride!'"

May and Harry didn't have children. They wanted children, but it never happened. Such a shame. They would have been wonderful parents. But as Harry always said, "It's not our job to question the Lord. He knows what's best for us. We just have to love each other more and love any stray children who need us."

Well, the Lord brought them strays. And not only the four-footed kind. But children with their parents, too. May and Harry opened up their old farmhouse to others. They turned no one away. They had picnics, Bible studies, song fests, prayer meetings, and so much more.

They created a community of believers led by the Lord. Once unruly children began to listen to their parents. Once frustrated parents began showing more love. And everyone grew in their faith. It was a special time of love and laughter. A time they thought would never end. But it did end as children grew up and went out on their own. As families left the farms. As life in this country changed. And then, of course, Harry died.

After Harry's passing, May sold off most of the farmland, but she couldn't part with their home because it housed her precious memories of their life together. She kept a few acres of land, which weren't good for farming. They were hilly with two creeks running through them. Beavers loved to make damns in the creeks. What a mess they made. They used to make Harry so mad! As he continually broke up the damns, the beavers started construction all over again. May was never quite sure who was the more stubborn, Harry or the beavers. They seemed to be an even match.

The groves sit right in the middle of the acres. A deep well is nearby. May prays it still works. Of course, they never removed the old outhouse. May wanted to, but Harry said,

"Oh, just leave it. You never know when you might need it." They laughed at the thought, but now May is glad it's still here.

The old windmill still stands intact, thanks to Harry. One day when she saw him out there working hard, she asked him, "Why are you doing that, Honey?"

"Because May Day, someday you're going to need this old windmill. The Lord told me so. It will look all worn out, but I'm going to make sure it will work. Nothing short of a tornado will take this down when I'm finished with it."

"Harry, what are you talking about?"

Harry stops what he's doing. He takes May's hands and looks directly into her blue eyes. "I don't want to scare you, but one day after I'm long gone, the Lord is going to call you to be strong. You'll come home to our old place, and you will lead other believers here. Don't worry, the Lord will be with you every step of the way as He has been all your life.

"Remember when we were deciding if we should get married?" May nods her head. "We said we'd pray about it and wait for the Lord's answer. We did. We prayed and we waited as we fell more and more in love."

"We didn't want to get married unless the Lord okayed it," says May.

"That's right, May Day. And He did. That morning, we were both at our own homes reading the same devotional reading. The Lord told each of us it was His will for us to marry. Remember the Bible verse He gave us?"

"Of course, Joshua 1:9: 'Be strong and courageous. Do not be afraid; do not be terrified, for the LORD your God will be with you wherever you go.'"

"Now let me get back to work, May Day. I must earn that good food you make for me." They both laugh.

That was so long ago. May didn't imagine she'd ever return to this sacred place, but something, or someone inside her told her not to sell the house. Maybe she remembered Harry's words. Maybe the Lord directed her. Probably both.

91

Anyhow, she's thankful she listened.

May

THE DAY THE WORLD CHANGED

May removes the key from the hiding place where it has been concealed for years; the secret compartment in her billfold. She puts it in the front door lock. It opens on the first try. As May walks in, memories flood her mind. Nothing has changed. Just more dust and cobwebs. Thankfully and remarkably, there are no signs of animals. This was a home filled with laughter and love. She feels the echoes of that love right now. It emerges around the corners and hugs her with limitless love, welcoming her home and comforting her.

A lifetime ago, she and Harry lived a happy, simple life here. He farmed and she made this big, drafty house a home. She had a huge vegetable garden and many flower gardens. She fed the farm cats that came and went from this place. When Harry had to walk with a cane, he'd grumpily comment, "Those dumb cats! I almost fell coming up the walk."

But as she secretly watched from the kitchen window, she saw him use his cane to pet each cat. They purred like little machines. May saw him smile at them. It was one of the many reasons she loved him.

In those days May baked bread from scratch almost every day. She made sure to have it baking when he came in from the field. He always said the same thing. "May Day, this place smells like heaven!" Then he'd lift her off her feet and "hug the stuffing out of her." His saying, not May's. Then they'd both laugh. A routine they never thought boring or repetitive.

Harry was the one who told May not long before he passed away, "God has big plans for you some day. I don't know what they are, but they're big. I know that it will be after I'm gone." A sad smile crosses his face. "I wish that I could be with you to help you, May Day. But always remember, the Lord loves you and He's always with you."

"Shush," May says as she grabs his hand. "You'll outlive both of us and we'll grow old together, living here the rest of our lives. I'll still be baking bread for you in my 90s and you'll still be lifting me off the ground!"

Harry was right about going first. May's not sure about God's big plans. After Harry was gone, she eventually felt the call to become a counselor. That was something she never imagined. The Lord knew what He was doing. In helping others, she helped herself.

And something else. In following the Lord's leading, May discovered the joy of walking with Him every single day, not just on Sundays. May's grief and sadness slowly left as she leaned into Him. As she leaned into the Lord, she wanted nothing more than to be His instrument on this earth.

This morning, a long-ago prayer returned to May. As a young person growing up in church, she loved the Prayer of St. Francis. It became a popular song when she was in youth group. She often sang the words: "Lord make me an instrument of your peace. Where there is hatred let me sow love. Where there is injury, pardon, Lord. Where there is doubt true faith in you..." It goes on to pray for hope in times of despair. Light in the darkness. And joy where there is sadness.

"O divine master grant that I may not seek to be consoled as to console; to be understood as to understand, to be loved as to love. For it is in giving that we receive. It is in pardoning that we are pardoned. And it's in dying that we are born to eternal life. Amen."

May realizes that this song has become her lifelong prayer. She's asked the Lord time and time again to make her an instrument of His peace.

Right now, at this moment, May feels a little tingle throughout her body. It's as if she knows that the plans God has for her will soon be revealed. Maybe His revelation is beginning today.

Another thought comes to May. The realization that peace always comes at a price. Peace is never easy. Peace is not giving in to lies. Peace is taking a bold stand for truth. God's truth. To be a true and godly peacemaker, one must endure heartache and trials.

"Oh, boy," thinks May. "What have I been praying for all these years? What have I gotten myself into?"

Ray and Molly

THE DAY THE WORLD CHANGED

May realizes she's been woolgathering. She steps aside to allow the others in. Quietly, each person is lost in their own thoughts, knowing that this will be their home for now. Maybe for the rest of their lives on this earth. If they're lucky.

They go their separate ways and find a place to call their own. Molly leads husband Ray to the cellar.

"Why all the way down here?" asks Ray in a grumpy voice. He's not as spry as he once was. Oh, he can still crawl around under sinks, but it's challenging to get back up, almost a Herculean task.

"Because, silly, you're a plumber. You can watch over the pipes. They're old. They need some TLC and you're the TPK."

"The what?" asks Ray, with no idea what his wife is talking about.

"The TPK," says Molly. She has a grin on her face. "The Pipe King." Ray smiles, a little, too. He never gets tired of her corny jokes.

"And," continues Molly, "I can make a home for us anywhere. You know that, Honey Bun," she says with her teasing smile.

Ray can't help himself. He smiles a big, wide smile. "It's true, Molly, you can. You have. And I'm thankful for that."

The first few years they were married they lived in his parents' basement. It was far from ideal. Yet, Molly made it special. When he came home after a long day of work, the basement looked like home, their home. Inviting aromas always emanated from the hotplate Molly used for cooking. And most of all, Molly was waiting with love in her heart just for him.

Ray's mother, Phyllis, was not an easy person to get along with as almost everyone in their small community could tell you. Many probably would if given the slightest opportunity. She was critical of others and a true perfectionist. No one ever accused her of exhibiting empathy or being overly kind.

And yet, Phyllis became the biggest Molly fan around. Molly made her mother-in-law feel like she was the Queen and that absolutely everyone adored her. It was easy for Molly since she sincerely respected Phyllis and truly loved her for many reasons. She was Ray's mother, after all. That was reason enough. And she did a good job of raising him. Molly will aways be thankful for that. But Molly also knew something else that was very special about her mother-in-law. She knew that Phyllis was a beloved daughter of the King, the same King she serves, Jesus Christ.

Grumpy Ray realizes a truth in this memory. There is no better wife, no better person than his Molly. Maybe there is something to be said for her belief in God. Maybe this God is real. "I just might have to look at one of those Bibles," he tells himself, wondering where that thought came from.

Pearl

THE DAY THE WORLD CHANGED

Even though Pearl is the oldest in the group, she works just as hard as everyone else. Frank looks at her and smiles with compassion and concern, "Should you be carrying that, Miss Pearl?" he asks.

"I grew up on a farm," says Pearl, who's still wearing her blue apron and pearls. "I'm used to hard work. Carrying a few supplies won't kill me. In fact, I need to be needed. It's the way I grew up. And I'm too old to change." Pearl smiles.

"I think you'll outlive us all, Miss Pearl," says Frank. "You remind me of my Aunt Elsie. She was always the first one up in the morning and always the last one to go to bed at night. I spent many summers at her farm. She worked harder than anyone else. But if I ever commented on all her hard work, she simply shooed me away, always saying the same thing. 'Now leave me alone, Franky. I have much to do today and little time to do it. Be a good boy and fetch some wood for this old wood burning stove and later I'll bake your favorite cookies.' I've never tasted a better sugar cookie than my Aunt Elsie's."

Pearl smiles. "She sounds like good people."

"Oh, the best," says Frank. "She was almost 100 years old when she went to sleep one night. When she wasn't up by sunrise, we thought that for the very first time in her life she'd overslept. But she wasn't oversleeping. She was having breakfast in heaven. Probably telling some of the angels what they had to get done that day." Frank chuckles.

Pearl chuckles, too. "She sounds like my kind of gal."

"Even though we've just met, I can tell that you're just like her, Miss Pearl."

"I'll take that as a great compliment, Frank. And my favorite cookie is a good sugar cookie, too."

They smile at one another with the realization that they are kindred spirits.

As they bring blankets and food through the groves, Jonah says to his mom, "It smells like Christmas inside here." They are surrounded by dozens of Blue Spruce trees. Too many to count.

Daisy takes a deep breath and smiles a sad smile, missing her husband, worrying about his safety. "It sure does," she says. "Just like Christmas Day."

As if he can read her thoughts, Jonah asks, "What's going to happen to Dad?"

"Oh, Honey, I don't know. I pray that the Lord will keep him safe. But we know we're living in the end times, right?"

Jonah nods his head "Yes."

"When the hearts of many grow cold and they don't believe in God. And because they don't believe in our Lord, they will do whatever they want. They will do evil things. They don't care about others, especially us believers. In fact, they hate us."

Both stop and to consider her words.

"Have you been praying for Dad?" asks Daisy.

"I have," says Jacob. "I prayed the whole way out here. And I'm going to keep on praying."

"Your dad would be so proud of you. He's always been

proud of you, Jonah."

The others haul the supplies inside.

Each person remembers their own happy Christmases. They are different and the same. Different traditions, but all spent with loved ones. Each one wonders what this next Christmas will hold. If Christmas will even arrive for them. Each one thinks about loved ones and wonder where they are and what is happening to them.

Pearl

THE DAY THE WORLD CHANGED

Pearl remembers life on the farm with her brothers and her mom and dad. A good life where they did their chores because it was expected. They never thought to question why. Pearl and her mom cooked, cleaned, raised chickens, and kept a big garden while the men worked the farm. They also made all their own clothes. They kept the fabric scraps and used them to make many quilts over the years.

For a moment Pearl thinks of all the beautiful quilts she had to leave behind. She's sad at the loss, but then remembers her mom's words.

"Pearl, the gift of sewing is a simple gift, but not everyone has it. Always be grateful for all the gifts the Lord has given you. Never take them for granted. Use them to help others.

"One of your best gifts is your ability to bounce back, Pearl. It's okay to be sad for a while, but don't make it a habit. With the Lord, brighter days are always coming."

Pearl misses her mom every day, but today she misses her more than ever. She was a woman of great wisdom. If Pearl had a problem, her mom always helped her find the solution.

Not by telling her what to do, but by guiding her with the words of the Bible.

"Sometimes we have to wait a long time for those better days," her mom told her more than once. "But they always arrive. Never forget that, Pearl."

Pearl smiles to herself. "I'm waiting for those better days, dear Lord."

Then another memory comes to Pearl. Her mom is speaking again. "Pearl, another gift you have is bringing people together. It's as if you take the scraps of their lives and make them part of the most beautiful quilt. One that is much better because they are part of it."

Pearl smiles at the memory. "Yes, I have made some lovely quilts in my day, but they're never as good as quilting people together, especially when they meet the Lord and become part of His quilt. His quilt is made of the most beautiful family of all because we all belong to Him.

"Thank you, Lord, for this new family," says Pearl. "Help us, dear Lord. Lead us and guide us. Stitch us together as one family. Your family. Just as the people of Israel traveled through the wilderness under your leading, lead us through this wilderness of hate and unbelief in a country that has forgotten you.

"How can they forget you, oh Lord? I guess just like in the days of Noah, people are doing what they see as right in their own minds. They don't think of you at all. Lord, protect us. May this makeshift family grow in our faith. Bless our fellowship, dear Lord. Strengthen us for this journey, Father God. I pray this in Jesus' mighty name. Amen."

Heather and Ben

THE DAY THE WORLD CHANGED

Heather and Ben carry supplies up to the house. They are still amazed at how well hidden the house is from view. A grove of trees exists within a grove of trees. As they walk inside the inner grove, Heather stops in her tracks.

"What is it, Heather?" Ben asks.

"Look, Ben," she says. "Look." She points to the house.

The white, two-story farmhouse is a pretty typical sight with one exception. There are red lines all over the house that look like veins.

"What is that?" asks Ben.

"That's Virginia Creeper. It's very invasive and looks as if it's been growing here for years," says Heather. "They always turn this color red in the fall."

"It looks like they have berries," Ben says hopefully.

"We can't eat them," says the Heather, the horticulturist. "They're poisonous." She pauses and then asks Ben, "Do they remind you of anything?"

"What do you mean?"

"Remember in the Bible when the spies went into Jericho

105

and Rahab the prostitute helped them?"

"Sure. And they told her to let the scarlet rope down outside the window where she helped them escape."

"Think about it, Ben. There's a scarlet cord running throughout the entire Bible. This Virginia creeper makes me think of it. God's love and mercy are evident throughout all the Bible stories. From the Old Testament to the New, God continually makes a way in the wilderness."

"The wilderness after they left Egypt," says Ben. "The wilderness in people's hearts living without hope. There are so many of those people now more than ever before. We're definitely in the wilderness now, Heather."

"So true. So true. Who knows what will happen to us? To anyone who's a true believer? But I have this intense feeling that this red is a sign to us."

"I can see that now," says Ben. "His blood on the cross covered our sins. When He rose from the dead, we know that He defeated death."

"Which is separation from God," says Heather.

"Boy, that's true!" says Ben. "Jesus' blood is a part of us now because we are born again believers. His blood covers this house. It's our place of safety because He's here with us."

"And just like Rahab becomes part of Jesus' family, we are all a part of God's family, too. We're grafted in. He will protect us. We are safe here."

"Thanks for sharing that, Heather. I believe it's true. It gives me hope."

The accountant and the horticulturist smile warmly at each other. Both wondering what the Lord has in store for them. Not only separately, but also together.

Ben looks at Heather. He sees her cherry red hair and especially notices her beautiful smile. "It's like sunshine itself," Ben thinks to himself.

Ben compares himself to Heather and he smiles. "I'm just a weed standing in her presence. She's like a wild daisy growing in a field. She's both delicate and resilient, unassuming, and beautiful. But she doesn't even know it," Ben thinks. "Yet, she also has a strength that cannot be easily taken from her. I can feel it. She's like a beautiful flower blooming against all odds in a windblown desert with no water. It shouldn't survive, but somehow it not only survives, it thrives.

"Lord, because you made a way in the wilderness for your people, I know that you can make a way for a flower and a weed to become true friends. Please make a way for Heather and me, Lord, as friends and maybe even more, if it's your will. Amen."

All this time Heather is watching Ben. She thinks to herself, "He has such a nice smile." Somehow, she knows he's a very special guy.

The Charlies

THE DAY THE WORLD CHANGED

The Charlies stand close together, holding hands so tightly that husband Charlie thinks all the blood has drained from his hand. A stern judge sits on an elevated chair. If it wasn't such a serious situation, Charlie would laugh at the absurdity of a small man garbed in voluminous robes sitting in what is essentially a highchair.

Armed guards flank both sides of the room. Staring into space, they're not seeing anything but they're ready and waiting to act, like guard dogs on high alert.

The judge clears his throat in a self-important way.

"Pastor Charlene Marie Pasture and Charlie Oliver Pasture you are being detained under the Anti-Hate Law. You are charged with being Haters. Our President declared we will no longer tolerate Haters in this great country. They undermine everything we believe in.

"Before you answer my next question, I must warn you. All Haters who refuse to renounce their so-called God and take the loyalty mark today will be executed immediately. On the other hand, all Haters who do renounce their God will be met with leniency and forgiveness. After all, we're not the monsters." The judge smiles a horrible smile. "The Haters are the monsters.

"What is your plea? Are you guilty of being Haters? Are you willing to renounce your God? Speak! I don't have all day!"

Charlie cannot speak. His mind is racing. Sweat soaks his clothes. He finds it difficult to breathe. An intense pressure seems to continue building in his chest. Just as he's afraid that he might pass out, Charlie feels his wife's hand squeeze his. Then his Sweet Charlie removes her hand.

An intense chill takes over Charlie's hand and travels throughout his entire body. He begins shaking uncontrollably.

His wife looks at him, mouthing the words, "I love you, Dear Charlie." She smiles her sweet smile that she saves only for him, then she steps forward.

Looking directly at the judge she does not waver. In fact, a look of peace washes over her. Charlie can see it. He can even feel it. In fact, everyone in the room feels the peace as if it's a physical substance. The guards and the judge pause, but don't understand. But Pastor Charlie's people know what this feeling is. Several of them start humming, "Surely the presence of the Lord is in this place. I can feel His mighty power and His grace. I can hear the brush of angels' wings; I see glory on each face. Surely the presence of the Lord is in this place."

Pastor Charlie looks directly at the judge and says calmly, "I am not a Hater, but I am a follower of my Lord and Savior Jesus Christ. He died for me and if necessary, I will gladly die for Him."

Her voice becomes louder and stronger. "No, I do not renounce my faith in Jesus Christ of Nazareth. In fact, I praise His holy name! The name above all names. One day at the mention of His name every knee shall bow, and every tongue shall confess that Jesus is Lord of lords and King of kings!"

Her voice fills every nook and cranny of the courtroom. It

takes up all the space inside every ear present.

Charlie shakes his head. He's sure that for just a moment he sees a white, bright light surrounding her. It's exactly like the light in his dream. After his mother died, he dreamed he was in a long hallway filled with the most beautiful light.

"I've never seen anything like this on earth," Charlie thinks to himself in the dream. Then in the middle of the hallway he sees someone step into the light. Looking closer, he knows he should recognize the person. It's as if they are a part of the light. He looks harder. The person smiles. Immediately, Charlie knows who it is, his beloved mom. She had the sweetest smile, and she also had a faith that never wavered.

The Lord was allowing Charlie a rare glimpse into heaven; he's sure of it. When Charlie wakes from his dream, he's encompassed by an incredible peace. The same peace that he knows his Sweet Charlie is experiencing right now. And Charlie knows without a doubt that this light surrounding his Sweet Charlie must be a light from God the Father Himself.

The courtroom erupts in applause. Pastor Charlie's church people are there waiting for their own sentencing. They're shouting the name of Jesus over and over. "Jesus! Jesus! Jesus!"

It becomes a holy chant, louder and louder. "Jesus! Jesus! Jesus!" People are jumping in the air with their hands held high toward heaven. "Jesus! Jesus! Jesus!" Singing breaks out. Praise and worship songs. "Amazing Grace," and "What a Friend We Have in Jesus" is among them.

The guards cover their ears, as if the mere mention of the name Jesus injures them beyond repair.

The judge climbs down from his high chair. Standing up as tall as he can, he pounds his gavel with all his strength. In fact, at one point he uses both hands at once as if he's pounding a nail into wood.

"You're out of order! Out of order!" he yells at Pastor Charlie. "Stop it right now! You're out of order! Guards, take this woman away! Execute her immediately!"

The guards, still stunned, are unable to move. They want to move. They want to obey their superior, but their feet are like cement. And their hands are immobilized. Their heads won't move. Their eyes are frozen staring straight ahead. Even their tongues don't work.

The judge leaves the front of the courtroom. Grabbing one of the guard's guns, he aims it directly at Pastor Charlie, who shows no fear. In fact, she is radiant. Not only does she glow, there's an undeniable light surrounding her. As the judge pulls the trigger everyone sees it. Even the guards who can suddenly move their heads and their eyes see the light.

At the instant the bullet hits Pastor Charlie, before she reaches the ground, a bright light shoots out of her like a rocket and travels to the ceiling. It looks like a trail.

"A trail to heaven," Charlie says out loud. "Leading her to her Lord."

Those church members close by hear Charlie and agree. "A trail to heaven. Our Pastor Charlie is going home!"

Charlie

THE DAY THE WORLD CHANGED

At the sound of the gun, the courtroom becomes as silent as a tomb. Many eyes still follow the white light surrounding Pastor Charlie and exiting through the ceiling. For a few short seconds, which seem like an eternity, no one moves. No one speaks. Pastor Charlie lies on the floor, looking strangely radiant even though she's obviously dead.

Eventually, order is restored in the courtroom. The judge regains his composure. With the help of one of the guards, he climbs back up onto his chair. The guards take their positions again. Their mobility restored, they line up perfectly in a row like a child's tin soldiers ready for a make-believe battle, although nothing about this scene is from a child's imagination. And nothing is make-believe. Each soldier stares into nothingness once again, the same nothingness that fills their souls.

Tired, the judge clears his voice and says, "Is there anyone in this courtroom with the good sense to renounce your so-called God? If so, step forward now or receive the same sentence as your Pastor."

No one moves forward. In fact, no one moves at all. They're all thinking about the light. They still feel the presence of the Holy Spirit all around them.

Eventually, the people are quietly removed from the courthouse. One woman guard with perfect posture, noisy heels, obviously dyed hair, and a stern countenance, has an odd expression on her face. It's one of almost reverence. As if she's on a holy mission as she helps to lead the others to their death.

Every single believer goes without protest, with one exception.

At the last minute, Charlie woodenly steps forward as if someone else is moving his feet with an invisible string. Looking directly at the judge, he says "I'm willing to renounce my faith."

Charlie's voice sounds strange to him, as if someone else is speaking.

Surprised at how easily he betrayed his wife, not to mention his God, Charlie recognizes the sad truth. His faith is shallow and weak, at best. It isn't a true, mature faith. In fact, he mistakenly thought that his Sweet Charlie's deep faith would save him, too. That's the real, tragic truth.

"Good. One smart man," says the judge. "Take him to re-education camp. Kill the rest and order my lunch. A club sandwich with extra mayo and those curly fries. I'm starving."

The judge slams his gavel one last time.

As he is escorted from the building, Charlie sees his wife's body among a large pile of bodies in the alley way, awaiting disposal. His memory flashes back to the piles of murdered Jews outside the concentration camps during World War II. It's a truth that is no longer taught, discussed, or even believed to be true. Yet, it is still horrifically true. The Holocaust happened and the world witnessed unleashed evil in a time that we swore we'd never forget and certainly never repeat.

"But people have forgotten," thinks Charlie. "How can this be happening?" he asks no one. Tears invade Charlie's eyes and overflow without warning like a tsunami that grows underneath the ocean undetected until it's too late to sound the alarms.

The sound of the judge's gavel slamming one last time rings in Charlie's ears. It reminds him that another will judge him one day. And he knows what he is. Guilty. Guilty. Guilty!

May

THE DAY THE WORLD CHANGED

"In a way," thinks May. "I'm the lucky one. If there is such a thing as luck, which I've never seen mentioned in the Bible. Mom used to always say that there's no such thing as luck. There's hard work and there's the Lord's intervention.

"But I am lucky in an odd way," May thinks. "I've already lost the most important person in my life, Harry. It's been long enough now that although I still miss him, the wounds have healed over and have become scars. I think of them as friendly scars. What once hurt so dramatically, has now simply become part of who I am.

"At a time like this, though, some of the pain pops out. There will always be a sliver in my heart. An empty spot that misses Harry. But these people are going through the not knowing what's happening right now. They have no idea what will happen to their loved ones. They are living in an episode of The Twilight Zone. Anything can happen. Nothing's off limits. What once was thought impossible is now living in the realm of possibility and maybe even probability.

"Their lives have already changed forever, even though they

may not admit it. They're already grieving without realizing it. The shock itself is covering up the grief for now. They can still pretend everything will go back to normal. But normal drove the truck down the road, into the next county, and off a steep hill. Normal has packed its bags and left the country without leaving a forwarding address. Normal is never coming back."

And May knows without a doubt that the Lord has called her in this very moment for such a time as this.

"Help me, dear Lord, to comfort your people," May prays. "Direct my steps. Give me Your words to speak over them. Give me your strength. I have no strength of my own. Amen."

May and the Others

PRESENT TIME

May feels it almost immediately. Everyone in this household woke up on the wrong side of the bed. Footsteps are too heavy. No one is walking calmly but banging around. Even the children, the most resilient of all, sound whiny and out of sorts.

Frank comes down the stairs and looks at her with his eyebrows raised.

"You noticed it, too?" she asks.

Frank simply nods his head in agreement. Never one to seek out conflict, Frank's first instinct is to hide. Instead, he says, "What can we do? There has to be something we can do."

"You gather them up and I'll put on the coffee. I have a surprise."

After much grumbling and fussing, everyone is sitting in the large living room, which extends into the dining room. The kids are sitting on the floor. Some of the younger adults, too. Molly and Frank hand out coffee and bring out the last of the hidden cookies as if they're gold. They might as well be.

There's a hush in the room. All eyes are on May.

"We got a new letter." And in that instant the grumpy mood changes to anticipation and hope.

"Read it! Read it!" they all say like school children.

"I will. I will," assures May. "But first, let's pray. Frank. Will you lead us?"

Frank nods his head as he bows.

"Most Loving Heavenly Father,

"We thank you for the provision you give us. You meet our daily needs, and you watch over us. We are yours, dear Lord. The sheep of your field. Members of your flock. We thank you for sparing us.

"Lead and guide each one of us here today and for all the days we have left on this earth. Lord, as we read another letter, fill us with your hope, your love, and your peace. Protect those who write these letters and those who deliver them. Bless them that they are your instruments working in these desperate times. Direct their steps and direct ours as well.

"Thank you for your remnant, Lord. Thank you that we are counted among them. We love you and we praise your holy name. We pray this all in Jesus' name, our Lord and Savior. Amen."

May nods her head in approval. "Thank you, Frank. That was beautiful."

Molly wipes her eyes as does Ray, who pretends to cough. He thinks the cough covers his emotion, but everyone knows the truth.

For the very first time, Molly thinks to herself, "I wonder if he's ready to commit to you, Lord." She looks at Ray and he smiles, as if he knows what she's thinking. Molly cries tears of joy. Ray hugs her reassuringly.

"I'll just read it," says May.

Dear Oliver,

By now you know who I am and whose I am. I am a daughter of the Most High King. And I know that you are His son. That makes us brother and sister. Well, Brother, He has set us in this place for such a time as this. We must get busy.

We don't know how long it will be before the Lord comes back to take His church home. We are called to reach out to the remnant in hiding. The Lord has assured me that the numbers are much more than we realize. Our fellow sheep need reassurance and guidance. We are to become a network of those working together for His plans. We now live in a hostile country and an even more hostile world. But His people are everywhere. We're not alone. We mustn't lose hope.

So, in this dark time, we must arm ourselves with the Lord's full armor. Never forget, not even for one moment, that we are not fighting against flesh and blood. Our fight is against the rulers, authorities, and powers of darkness. We must take our stand against the devil himself. We can't do it alone. With God, we are never alone. He is our strength and our high tower. We run to Him and He saves us.

We must buckle the belt of truth around our waist. We must never give in to the lies. Lies don't come from God. He is truth. We must put the breastplate of righteousness in place. It covers our heart and keeps us loyal to the Holy One.

We firmly place the helmet of Salvation on our heads. We know that Jesus died for us. We ask Him to protect our minds from the devil who wants to make us doubt our Lord.

We hold tight to the Shield of Faith to ward off the fiery darts of the evil one. He wants us to believe that the Lord has abandoned us. He wants us to look at our present circumstances and forget about our true home in heaven.

We slip on the Shoes of Peace with the readiness to share the Gospel with those who do not know it or have purposefully ignored it. There are so many who don't know our Lord. They are deceived and they are unaware of what is on the line. Their very souls! We take every opportunity the Lord provides to share the Good News!

And we must hold unrelentingly to the Sword of the Spirit,

which is the Word of God. God's Word leads us and guides us. We don't have to be afraid even though we are living in terrifying times. God's got this. He's with us. He'll never leave us or forsake us.

So, dear brother, as they used to say to those who were sauntering through life, "Let's get the lead out!" Let's look for those opportunities the Lord provides and move forward into battle!

It makes me want to sing, "Onward Christian soldiers! Marching as to war, with the cross of Jesus going on before. Christ the royal Master, leads against the foe; forward into battle, see, His banners go! Onward Christian soldiers, marching as to war, with the cross of Jesus going on before!"

Instead, I close with hope and marching orders from our Lord and our King. Let's get the lead out! Let's read God's Word. Let's pray for direction. Always pray.

Love, Alphie

At first, no one speaks. Each person is lost in their own thoughts. How will the Lord call them to action? What can they possibly do? Who is this Alphie?

Then Molly looks at Ray. Her big, strong, and stoic Ray is sobbing. She puts her arms around him and tries to comfort him.

Ray smiles at her through his tears. "It's okay, it's okay, Molly. Let me speak."

Everyone turns toward Ray, wondering what this man of few words will say. He clears his throat. "I've always been pretty self-sufficient. I had a good life growing up, but it was also hard. My parents loved each other and loved us, but they were people of few words. I guess I've been the same way." He grins and looks at Molly. Who nods her head "Yes."

"Maybe it was because they didn't know the Lord. They came from a long line of unbelievers down many generations. It's not that they were atheists. Or set out to be unbelievers.

They just didn't think about God enough to purposefully not believe in Him. It was all they knew.

"They didn't have any examples in the family to follow. No one had God in their lives so they couldn't talk about Him. They couldn't tell of all the great things He'd done because they never accepted Him or believed in Him.

"That was until the day that my Molly brought them to the Lord. She told them her testimony about how Jesus came into her life and completely changed her. Then, both my mom and dad asked Jesus to be the Lord of their lives, too. They dramatically changed after that. And I know without any doubt that they're both in heaven today.

"And now, more than ever, I'm so thankful for my Molly." Tears run down Ray's cheeks. "I wouldn't listen to her back then, but I know that she's been right all along. And I know that she's never stopped praying for me.

"But I want you to know that today, I'm changing. Today I'm giving my life to the Lord. I know He exists, and I know He loves me. It's hard to explain, but somehow, He told me so as May was reading the letter. I just want all of you to know.

"I guess we're family now and I don't want any secrets. I asked the Lord to forgive me for my sins. I know He died on the cross for me and after three days rose from the dead. My Molly has told me enough times." Molly and Ray laugh.

"I feel a whole lot lighter. I feel ... amazing!"

In unison, Jonah, Beth, and Erin shout, "Party time!" Jonah elaborates. "They're throwing a party in heaven for you right now, Ray. It says so in the Bible."

"That's right!" says Molly. "I think it's in Luke 15:7. Jesus says, 'There will be more rejoicing in heaven over one sinner who repents than over ninety-nine righteous people who have no need of repentance.'"

"That's what we said," says Erin. Then all three children chime in again. "Party time!"

Alphina

PRESENT TIME

At times when Alphina is sitting in Room 33 in the BHU, her mind wanders. It's no surprise, since she cannot physically travel outside her room. Sometimes her mind travels to places it's never been. Sometimes the Lord speaks to Alphina in her heart, and she listens. Sometimes, she simply remembers.

Today, something she wrote long ago comes back for a visit, all at once. It doesn't politely knock on the door; it pushes the door down with its big boots and enters like it owns the place. Alphina laughs a little in the anticipation of remembering. She welcomes the words she wrote so very long ago like a cherished old friend. Words that serve her well today just like they did back then.

The Girl in the Mirror
Sometimes I look into the mirror, and I wonder, "What happened to that young girl from so long ago?" So fresh and ready to live life new every day and conquer fears that always try to stand in the way.

Where is that girl who simply loved the Lord and believed

everything she learned in Sunday School? There were no questions or doubts, only faith with joy.

What happened to that girl with the big dreams? The one who wanted to drive across the country and stop wherever the road took an interesting turn. She wanted to meet new people and write down their stories. And in doing so, she hoped to understand her own story a little better.

Where is the girl who wanted to find love that would last a lifetime with someone who wanted adventure, too? To spend life getting to know that other person as they went from one big adventure to the next.

Where is that girl who wanted to travel to far off lands and see firsthand different cultures and unique people? And discover the truth. Are people half a world away the same as a girl who grew up next to the sound of growing corn? Do they have the same hopes in their lives? The same dreams? Or do they dream differently in strange lands? Strange only because the young girl does not know them.

Where is that girl now? The one who never saw barriers but only saw opportunities. The one who dove into change like others dive into the calm waters in the public swimming pool. As they're quickly coming up for air, she's diving the fourth, fifth and sixth time into the waters of change.

I know that girl is still there, buried under life, but waiting for the right time to reappear. Older? Yes. Wiser? Hopefully. And yet, she's been here all along. She's changed and she's stayed the same. Isn't that the story of each life? We change. We stay the same. We become the people we've always been.

As she ages, the girl in the mirror finds she's still conquering fears. Some are the same. Some are very different. She wrestles them to the ground, but only with the help of the Lord. Somewhere along the way she discovers an important truth: wrestling with the Lord is not the answer, because He is the answer. And she learns once again to simply trust in Him.

The fears? She kicks them to the side of the road as she

leaves them in her dust. It's funny that as one is gone another appears; like in a B-rated sci-fi movie where the cardboard set falls over and you see the wires attached to a flying creature. You think the bad guy is gone until he morphs into another bad guy. And you realize a truth. If you're living life, there's always going to be a little bit of fear, but fear doesn't have to win.

That young girl who wanted to travel has traveled the farthest distance of all. Not to foreign lands, well a couple. But the farthest distance she's gone is to step outside herself and meet other people where they are and appreciate them for who they are. Sometimes she's even stepped onto their path and joined them in the journey they're on. She's traveled to their stories and learned to hear the words they do not speak. And she has written their stories. Some of them she's even written on her heart. That's where they still live today.

The girl in the mirror has found love for a lifetime even if the person she loved is no longer on this earth. But what a blessing to have had that love. And what a blessing to love so many people right now who are part of God's family.

The girl in the mirror discovers that, as we grow older, change is our constant companion. Now she wishes change would not be such a good friend. She wishes change would be a distant cousin she sees once a decade and hugs awkwardly. But the girl laughs to realize that what she always wanted she already has. That realization has only happened through change the Lord has directed.

She simply loves the Lord, who has been with her through this journey we call life. He's held her hand, given her joy, and helped her to step into adventures that even she couldn't dream up. If we can look into the mirror and see Him reflected in our in our image, then we are living the best adventure of all. A life of love that begins and ends and begins again with the Lord.

Charlie

PRESENT TIME

Charlie's working again. He doesn't do much else. After re-education camp, the authorities decided this was the perfect assignment for him. They obviously weren't going to let him teach again. And schools have changed dramatically. The emphasis is no longer on the basics. The basics have changed. There are no history or literature classes. Those in power are rewriting history and literature is considered too inflammatory.

Math and reading are still taught, but the main classes are physical education and indoctrination. They have a new Pledge of Allegiance, but it's not to this country. And it certainly doesn't mention God. No, it's The Pledge of Allegiance to the Global Society.

"I pledge allegiance to the Global Society for which we must all stand. One global unified society where we live in peace and harmony without borders. No longer ruled by Haters, we stand together for freedom as the Global Society defines it. We are indivisible with liberty, justice, and truth for all."

Charlie memorized this pledge during his months of indoctrination. He learned it very well. To say the words were beaten into him is putting it mildly. Every time someone misspoke even one word, they were whipped.

More than once, Charlie thought of Jesus on the night in which He was arrested even though he had done nothing wrong. They beat Him, too. On the day of His crucifixion, He was beaten 39 times with a cat of nine tails. That means flesh was ripped and torn from His body with every lash.

In Roman law 40 lashes is considered lethal. You see, they didn't want Jesus to die too soon. They wanted Him to suffer. That was the whole idea behind crucifixion. It was not a kind, easy, or quick way to die.

Charlie is ashamed to think of what Jesus went through for him and how easily he, Charlie, crumpled in fear. It's amazing that Charlie made it out of the re-education camp alive, but he wonders, "Is this really living?"

Charlie has a room of his own and three meals a day. He knows exactly where the cameras are hidden in his room and all around the hospital. He's very cautious to always appear to be working hard when he's at work and to be doing nothing at all when he's in his room.

He should be happy. He's alive, after all. Most of those he knew and loved are not. He doesn't have a home, a car, or a bank account to worry about. Charlie's money was seized immediately. His home and car were taken away and given to a deserving family. He doesn't know who. He only knows they are true patriots, unlike him. Charlie can never erase the fact that his wife was a believer. Even though he professed no real faith, he will never be completely trusted.

It still nags at him. His betrayal. He betrayed everything he thought he believed in. He betrayed his own wife, Sweet Charlie. She was willing to die rather than renounce her faith. Even with all their various brainwashing methods, they couldn't take this fact from him. A part of him wishes they could. But another part believes it's his price to pay for loving one of them. The Haters. Even as he thinks it, he knows it's not true. His Sweet Charlie was the most loving person he ever knew. So kind and giving, she hated no one. She simply loved the Lord. How can that be wrong? And she loved Charlie so well.

As he mops the floor for the thousandth or ten thousandth time, his thoughts turn back to happier moments like meeting Charlie for the first time at the coffee bar at church. She came flying past him, her long, curly, bright cherry red hair flying in 40 directions at once. She almost knocked him over getting to the coffee. She was horrified. He was enthralled. Her presence was undeniable. She apologized. He asked her out for lunch. Sometime between the meal and the dessert he knew he was going to marry this woman. It was the smartest decision he ever made. They were so ridiculously happy together.

One day, not long before the world changed, Charlie was looking across the breakfast table at his Sweet Charlie. They had just finished their devotions together when a thought entered Charlie's mind. "We are so ridiculously happy. I better cherish this time."

Was that the Lord nudging him to relish and be grateful for his life with his Sweet Charlie before it all changed? Charlie wonders.

He shakes his head. He spends too much time daydreaming of the good old days. Days that will never come again. The way of life that's long gone. A sadness sweeps over him like flood waters. He lets out a big sigh as deep as the ocean and twice as wide.

He could easily get lost in this sadness, but he knows he must not. Why? He's not sure. He has an indescribable feeling that he's meant for more. Much more. But what that might be, or when it might happen, he has no idea.

He only knows he absolutely cannot give up, so he trudges on with his mop and bucket, cleaning hallways and rooms that others seldom visit except for himself, Charlie the Cleaner.

"Ha! Charlie the Cleaner," thinks Charlie. "I'm so dirty. I'll never truly be clean again."

Outside Alphina's room he's cleaning again, as always. And once again Alphina is typing her random series of numbers on the ancient black typewriter, humming the Alphabet Song over and over again. Charlie stops what he's doing. Once again, he has that disturbing feeling of being observed.

He looks at Alphina. She stops typing. She boldly watches him now as if she knows his thoughts. As if she remembers the time before the world turned upside down and inside out. As if she remembers him.

Charlie looks at her again. This time is different. As different as pink-and-white zebras and howler monkeys on drugs. This time, she looks back. This time, Alphina smiles. Charlie looks directly at Alphina. She opens her mouth, but no numbers come out. Instead, she speaks his name. "Charlie."

Charlie is in shock. Alphina knows his name. She said his name and not numbers. And she speaks his name as if she knows him. And not just a little, but very well. She said his name with affection.

That's not all she does. This harmless, little old lady with a few slices short of a loaf of bread, she mouths the word. The most forbidden word not only in this country but throughout the entire world. The name no one is allowed to speak. The name that will get you thrown into a prison cell without a key. Or worse. It will get you executed on the spot.

Alphina in the Behavioral Health Unit room number 33 speaks the outlawed, forbidden, riot-inducing, hated name. Alphina says, "Jesus."

Charlie falls to his knees. His first thought is: "The name above all names." Thankfully, he doesn't say this out loud. He struggles to stand up, but he makes it just in time to look at Alphina again. He doesn't know why he looks or what he expects to see. He only knows that he cannot help but look directly at her.

She smiles the most loving, the most coherent smile at him. She speaks again. She simply says, "The Charlies."

Charlie falls backwards as if someone slaps him in the face. He gets up and runs down the hall as if the devil himself is chasing him, shaking violently as fear encompasses his entire body.

In his mind he keeps repeating the word, "What! What! What!" Over and over. As if this mantra will erase what just happened. As if this pagan prayer-like repetition will take away the name spoken out loud.

As if it will ease the fact that Alphina knows Charlie's name and she knows so much more. She knows him. With a knowledge he can't understand, Charlie knows Alphina knows him and all that he used to be.

And more importantly, and much more dangerous, Alphina knows Jesus! How can that be? Isn't she crazy? Can crazy people know the Lord?

Then a terrifying thought enters Charlie's mind. "What if she's not crazy? What does that mean? And if she's not crazy and she knows who I am and who I used to be, what will happen to me?"

And for the second time in his life, Charlie experiences an anxiety attack. He can barely breathe. He feels like a guppy out of water. It feels like his heart will beat out of his chest and crash into the wall. His chest hurts just as he imagines it does with a real heart attack. It's exactly how he felt when his Sweet Charlie was murdered.

"Wait," thinks Charlie. "Wait! Alphina knows my Charlie, too. What! How is that even possible?"

Charlie takes deep breaths and tries to think about anything else. His Sweet Charlie's face comes to his mind. He always told her she had the face of an angel. Slowly, he calms down. Slowly, he breathes normally again. Slowly, a tiny flicker of hope ignites in his soul.

133

May and Frank

PRESENT TIME

The weather is changing. The greens of summer are changing into the beautiful colors of fall. They are subtle colors, but beautiful, nonetheless.

"What are you thinking?" asks Frank.

He and May have started taking walks together on the days Ben believes are relatively safe. At least there are no drones flying around, according to Ben's field research. Of course, Frank and May faithfully pray before going outside and they never go very far, just around the property.

"There's a crispness in the air. Have you noticed it? It's almost as if I can break off a piece of fall and eat it," May answers.

"Yes," says Frank. "It probably tastes like Pumpkin Spice." They smile at one another with the memory of a favorite fall flavor.

"Summer is over," May says. "Fall is in full swing. It won't be long before winter arrives. Are we prepared?"

Frank laughs. "I doubt it, but the Lord is. He's with us."

"If we know nothing else, we know that," says May.

May and Frank smile at each other again. It seems like they've known each other for many years, even though in chronological time, it hasn't been very long.

They round the bend, still inside the fortress of evergreen trees when May spots it. "Look, Frank! Another letter!"

Frank looks all around them and sees nothing out of the ordinary. They see no person or any tracks. Frank picks it up. "Let's take it inside right away and call everyone down to hear it."

"Great idea!" agrees May.

Inside the house Frank yells out, "Hey, Everyone! We've got a new letter! Let's meet in the living room right now."

Sounds of rushing footsteps come from every part of the house. Ray is the loudest as he emerges from the basement with his Molly in tow. "Hurry, Molly! Hurry!" yells Ray as he almost trips over his own feet. Molly laughs. "They won't start without us, Ray!" she says.

It doesn't take long for all the members of this makeshift family to gather. Each one sits comfortably in their favorite spot. Pearl chuckles to herself thinking, "We are such creatures of habit. We all have our favorite spot, just like the old family dog."

Her mind flashes back to an old border collie named Ralph. He was the best cow herder around. And he worked hard all his life. His favorite spot to sit was at Pearl's dad's feet. Her dad didn't say a lot, but he had a big presence. He sure loved his family and yes, he loved that old Ralph, too.

"Okay," says Frank. "Let's see what Alphie has for us today. Let's pray first. Dear Lord, we thank you for these letters. We know they come from you through Alphie.

"Protect Alphie and keep her safe. We have no idea how she's getting these messages out, but you know, Lord. Protect all who are involved in this endeavor. We can't go far, Lord, but wherever we are, direct our steps and make our paths obvious. Continue to lead us and guide us. We belong to you, dear Lord. Our very lives are in your hands. We praise you and we thank you. Amen."

Frank unfolds the letter. His roommates are silent with anticipation. It's a holy moment as if God Himself will be speaking directly to each one of them. There's an awe and reverence in the room.

Frank reads.

Dear Oliver,

Today I feel led by the Lord to share this story with you. As you now remember I'm sure, I was a writer in my other life. I haven't written for a very long time. But recently, the Lord has been bringing new ideas and new thoughts to my mind. This is something I feel He gave me. I'm also sure it isn't for me alone. It must have some significance for others as well. Please share it.

And as always, be careful. I'm praying for you, dear Oliver. I'm praying for the brave delivery people. And, of course, I'm praying for all the Lord's remnants. Dear Remnant, may the Lord be with you. May He make you strong because He is strong. May you always remember that the Lord is in control. And may each one of you know without any doubt that He loves you. Not only today and tomorrow, but He loves you in every season and for eternity!

The Little Daisy

In a land not far away, in a time not long ago, the Gardener looks at the rich, dark soil with hope. He has a plan. With great excitement he plants. First, he places wild mint in the middle of the garden. "This will smell sweet on hot summer days," he says. "When the wind blows and the birds sing songs of sadness, knowing summer doesn't last forever, they will be comforted."

Next, he plants plain green and white hostas. "These look plain now, but when they bloom their purple flowers will be a lovely surprise. Of course, they have that beauty within them always, but they don't know it. Neither do others looking at them now. But I know. That's all that matters."

Now he plants yellow and gold marigolds all around the perimeter. "Their smell will keep some animals away who might eat the other flowers. In the fall, their colors will shine brightly in the sun."

The Gardener looks at his garden and knows that it is good. Still, something's missing. "Ah," he says. "The daisies."

He plants white daisies in between all the other flowers. In full bloom, they're the shining bright spots of the entire garden. He loves all the plants, but the daisies make him smile.

Every day the Gardener walks by his garden and every day he encourages the flowers to grow. The wild mint grows with wild abandon. He likes to rub their leaves and release their sweet, minty aroma. The hostas grow so tall and so big he thinks they might shade the other plants, but they don't. They're polite that way.

Like soldiers, the marigolds bloom precisely where they are planted, all in a military-style row without deviating one bit. If they could sweep the entire garden and align the dirt in perfect order, they would. When animals stand nearby merely thinking about entering the garden, the marigolds, in perfect unison, send out their overpowering scent, warding off would-be attackers. They take their job, their calling, quite seriously.

And the daisies bloom.

Until one day when the Gardener notices that no new blooms are coming. All the daisy blooms are still the original ones. And they're all withering and dying. Looking closer he realizes that something has been attacking the daisies. He sees nibble marks. He sees stems on the ground around the daisies. Petals have not naturally fallen off to make way for the new. They've been yanked away. An enemy has gotten into the garden and has attacked every single daisy plant.

The marigolds are devastated. They have not done their job. But the Gardener reassures them that they've done what they are designed to do. Serve and protect. An enemy has infiltrated the garden when no one was looking. This was a bigger enemy than the marigolds can ward off. The Gardener knows this enemy too well. This enemy was once his friend.

The Gardener speaks to the daisies. He encourages them. He tells them not to give up. He waters them with special nutrients. They live, but sadly, they never bloom again.

The rest of the garden continues to grow and bloom. The hostas' purple blooms are magnificent. The wild mint smells sweeter than before. In the fall the marigolds shine like liquid gold in the sunlight. The flowerless daisies trudge on. The Gardener encourages them all. And, of course, he loves them.

Without warning, the weather turns on the garden. Too soon the fall weather abandons them, leaving the door wide open to winter. Winter marches in like he owns the place and brings with him bitter wind and cold temperatures. The garden shivers. They know it won't be long before they must sleep. The daisies are the first to go. Next the hostas lay down their purple blooms and rest on the ground. The mint, still smelling sweet, follows.

The marigolds refuse to leave their post until the Gardener tells them, "It's okay, guys. You've done a great job. Rest now. You deserve it. See you in the spring."

That's when he sees it. Hiding behind the fallen mint. A small daisy. Not sleeping, but blooming. The Gardener laughs. It's blooming out of season. It's blooming just for him. And the Gardener watches the little daisy bloom during days when the bitter wind thinks he's king. During days when the cold temperatures rule without mercy. Even during the first snowfall, the Little Daisy still blooms.

Finally, the Gardener says, "It's time, Little Daisy. You have bloomed well. You have loved well. Come home with me."

The Little Daisy looks up at the Gardener and smiles. The Little Daisy goes home with the Gardener to bloom forever in his special garden.

I hope this has special meaning to some or all of you. I

139

have a feeling the Lord is saying that we are all like the Little Daisy. We're in hiding now, but because of His great love for each one of us, we are still blooming out of season, for such a time as this, a time when it makes no sense to bloom. And yet, because we belong to the Master Gardener, we bloom.

So bloom well, my fellow believers. Bloom in the summer when the sun is hot and friendly, and worry is as far away as an ice storm in winter. Bloom in the fall when the leaves are the most beautiful right before they let go.

Bloom amid winter remembering that in every winter day there exists a small seed of Spring. And bloom in the Spring, when the Lord fills us with His hope and His love.

Bloom in His love no matter what season you're in because in every season the Lord is with those who belong to Him, who are called according to His purpose.

Love, Alphie

Charlie

PRESENT TIME

Charlie's back in his room, pacing back and forth, thinking, "How does she know me? How does she know me? How does she know Sweet Charlie?" Without realizing it, Charlie speaks out loud. "Lord, how does she know me?" It's a prayer he doesn't know he's praying, but one he's praying nonetheless.

As if the Lord is answering him immediately, Charlie sees a scene from his life flash in front of him. The scene is before all this craziness in which he now lives began. He sees a lovely woman filled with laughter and words. A woman who barely stops talking because she has so much to share. Words bubble out of her and overflow in a loving, encouraging way.

Charlie thinks of Psalm 23, specifically the part that reads, "My cup runneth over." Her cup runs over and over and over with the Lord's blessings. Charlie knows it's true as he remembers her. The woman in room 33, Alphina.

He struggles to remember something else. It seems so important. Then it comes to him all at once. A writer? That's right! A writer! Alphie the writer.

As if he's there right now, Charlie remembers her now.

He sees the pew where she sat in his Sweet Charlie's church service every Sunday. Full of life and full of love. Alphie treats everyone the same. Each one she meets is her best friend. No one is a stranger.

Now he remembers. They hear that she's been admitted to the Behavioral Health Unit at the local hospital. The doctors diagnose her with schizophrenia. No one in church can believe it. Not their Alphie who exhibits no signs of anything being wrong. In fact, she's about as nice and as normal as it gets. Charlie remembers telling his Sweet Charlie, "Alphie is the poster girl for normal and well adjusted."

Pastor Charlie agrees with her husband. She knows something is not right. She goes to the BHU and attempts to get Alphie released. They say she exhibits all the classic symptoms. The bottom line is, they say, she's staying. But those in charge allow Pastor Charlie to visit Alphie in her room. That's a miracle. They're very strict about visitors, especially ones who are connected to the Christian religion in any way.

Alphie is the name by which everyone in church calls Alphina. It was her family's nickname for her when she was growing up. It stayed with her. It suits her. She's sweet and whimsical. Also, a little flighty at times and very physically fit.

Pastor Charlie saw her more than once jump over the back pew into her seat. One day a parishioner asked Pastor Charlie why Alphie did that. "I don't know," said Pastor Charlie. "I just hope that when I'm her age I can do that, too. Although, I can't do it now so it would have to be a miracle." They both laughed.

Alphie's brothers always loved teasing her. Every chance they got they'd sing or say the words to that song, "What's it all about, Alphie?" The strange part was, they knew that Alphie usually knew what was really going on before anyone else. At times it was uncanny how she could predict some people's behavior.

There was the time they got a new pastor at their home

church. After the first sermon when everyone else was commenting on how well the pastor did, Alphie just shook her head. On the ride home, her brothers asked her, "What's it all about, Alphie?" They really wanted to know.

"That new pastor. He's going to be trouble." Alphie refused to elaborate and said no more. But in time they found out the truth. This pastor was trouble. He caused dissention among the church people. He caused opposing sides to form. Former friends became enemies. He upset that congregation in a way that had never happened before. Eventually, the church leaders asked him to leave, but not before he did a lot of damage.

Even though she was still a girl at home, Alphie knew the truth before anyone else. More and more Alphie's family came to believe that Alphie's gift was from God. The spiritual gift of discernment.

Pastor Charlie speaks with Alphie, all the while holding her hand.

Later, she tells her husband, "Surprisingly, Alphie's at peace. But it's not the resigned peace of someone settling into what must be. She's at peace because the peace is from the Lord. Charlie, I'll try to explain."

Pastor Charlie shares with her husband their whispered conversation.

"This is where I'm supposed to be, Pastor Charlie," Alphie told her. "It's easy for them to think there's something wrong with me. When I was a teenager, I was in one of these places for a short time. I was depressed. I don't know why. In looking back, I think it had to do with hormonal changes. But the doctor my parents took me to decided that I belonged here. He convinced my parents that it was necessary. I know they allowed it out of love and concern for me. I wasn't here long, but it's still on my record."

Pastor Charlie said nothing but continued holding Alphie's hand.

"I'm not really sick or crazy," Alphie continued. "But I am called. The Lord has placed me here for such a time as this. That's all I know. Except that life will change very, very soon. The country we know right now will no longer exist. Don't worry about that, just stay true to the Lord, Pastor Charlie. Stay true to Jesus."

Then Pastor Charlie tells her Charlie that Alphie started humming the alphabet song. And as he remembers all this, Charlie remembers something else. That day was the last time that Alphie spoke real words to anyone.

"Except for today," Charlie says out loud to no one.

Thinking more clearly than he has since his re-education, Charlie remembers other things he forgot. After his beloved Charlie spoke with Alphie, it was only a short time later that the President announced the Anti-Hate Law and began hunting Christians, whom he calls Haters. Just like in Nazi Germany when the Jews were belittled and dehumanized, so it is with the Haters.

Suddenly, being a believer in Jesus Christ is outlawed. Then the arrests and the mass murders. The re-education camps. Not all survived them, but Charlie did.

"Survived for what?" Charlie asks for not the first time. But this time, he receives an answer.

It's as if the Lord removes the scales from Charlie's eyes just like He did with Saul when he was on the road to Damascus so many centuries ago. A well-educated and respected member of the Sanhedrin, Saul was journeying to persecute more followers of The Way. What we call Christians today. The Lord spoke to him. He also temporarily blinded him. When Saul could see again, the scales of lies and deception also fell from his eyes. Suddenly, Saul could not only see the truth, he knew the truth, Jesus Christ. Saul became Apostle Paul and brought the Gospel message to the Gentiles.

"I'm nothing like Apostle Paul," Charlie tells himself. "But I know that the Lord Himself has given me my memory back."

Charlie not only remembers clearly, he now sees clearly. He sees the lies. He sees the truth. He knows the Truth. Jesus is the Way, the Truth, and the Life. And Jesus has set him free to live exactly in this moment. For such a time as this, as his wife, his Sweet Charlie always told him.

"No matter what happens in our lives, my Dear Charlie, don't be discouraged," his wife told him one day. "And don't question the Lord. He created us to live specifically during this time. We don't know why, but He created each of us for such a time as this.

"Just as He did with Queen Esther, we have a choice. Remember what Mordecai said to her? 'Don't think for a moment that because you're in the palace you will escape when all the other Jews are killed. If you keep quiet at a time like this, deliverance and relief for the Jews will arise from some other place, but you and your relatives will die. Who knows if you were made queen just for such a time as this?'

"Let's never do that. Let's never deny our Lord. I don't know what it means, but I know without a doubt, Dear Charlie, that soon and very soon we will realize that this is our time. Never forget that. Just trust in the Lord and allow Him to direct your steps.

"But if you find yourself all alone and you waver in your faith, come back, Dear Charlie. Come back home to the Lord. Remember what Jesus said to Peter? Peter was saying he would die with Jesus. But Jesus tells Peter that before the rooster crows, he will deny Him three times.

"He doesn't leave it there. Jesus finishes the prophecy by telling Peter that when he comes back from the denial, he should strengthen his brothers. He's saying Peter will return to the faith. And He's giving him a job. Help the others, strengthen them. Lead and guide them.

"Don't forget this, dear Charlie. Even if you falter, come back home. Strengthen your brothers and sisters. You were made for such a time as this."

Charlie the Cleaner says under his breath, "I'll try, Sweet Charlie.

I'll try."

Charlie

PRESENT TIME

It was a bright sunny day, and this morning Charlie awoke with a purpose. His dream last night was a rallying cry. In his dream he saw the wooden door with iron bolts. The one he saw so long ago in another dream. For the first time, he now sees that the door is behind an altar. He runs toward the door as fast as he can even though the door is bolted shut. Charlie knows without a doubt that the Lord will open it at just the right time. The dream ends while he's still running, but he glimpses something nailed to the door. Something small. Like a playing card. Maybe the King of Hearts? Charlie isn't sure, but when he wakes up, he knows what he must do.

Charlie removes the typewritten sheets from the walls in room 33. He goes straight to the head of the Peacekeepers, Brandon.

"Sir," Charlie begins, "I have an idea. I think it's time to clean Alphina's room. I'd like to do it, if you approve. I think she needs a new start. I know I appreciate the new start I've been given," Charlie holds his breath and silently prays.

Brandon looks him over for an unnervingly long time. Then

he says, "I think it's a good idea. Let me talk to my superiors. Wait here."

Charlie is left standing in Brandon's office. He continues to pray. "Lord, please lead me and guide me. I don't know what I'm doing, but you do. Show me the path you want me to take."

Brandon returns, smiling. "They agree," he says. "In fact, they appreciate your initiative. Frankly, it surprises all of us. We've always wondered about your allegiance, but this shows that you're more of a team player than we previously thought. Charlie, there just might be a future for you after all."

Charlie keeps looking at Brandon and never blinks, but woodenly smiles. He's playing the part well. And he knows from experience that you never turn your back on a junkyard dog.

What Brandon doesn't say is that they all think this shows there just might be a future for other former Haters, too. What an intriguing thought. They had pretty much given up on all of them. They keep them around mainly to do the menial tasks no one else wants to do. Maybe there is more that the former Haters can do. It's worth exploring.

And maybe a clean room for Alphina will give her a new start, too. Although no one who works in this locked ward believes that. Not the doctors, not the nurses, not the orderlies, or any of the other patients.

All agree on one thing. Alphina is beyond help. A nut case who's become more like a pleasant mascot than a person who's getting better. She seems so harmless to the authorities; they barely notice her anymore. That's her strength. That and the Lord God Almighty, of course.

Charlie, the former numbers guy, takes Alphie's sheets home to his room, which is on the same floor as the Behavioral Health Unit. He does what he does best. He deciphers them. He breaks the code. It's so simple, really. "I can't believe I didn't see this before," thinks Charlie.

1234567. ABCDEFG. The simplest of ciphers. That's why she's always singing that song around him. That's why she speaks only in numbers. Wow, what an incredibly patient woman.

He reads her messages. Each one begins, 4, 5, 1, 18; 15, 12, 9, 22, 5, 18. "Dear Oliver." Each one encourages the reader with the love of God. And each one is signed, 12, 15, 22, 5; 1, 12, 16, 8, 9, 5. "Love, Alphie."

Astounded, he knows the truth. Alphie may be one of the sanest persons living in this crazy, upside-down world. With a clarity he has not had for a long time, Charlie knows that this is his moment. This is why he's still alive. This is why he's working and living here. This is why the Lord spared him. He has called him to be here now for such a time as this.

"You can use me, Lord?" Charlie humbly asks. "Really? After all I've done." Then he remembers his Sweet Charlie's words. "When you come back to the Lord, don't beat yourself up, Dear Charlie. That doesn't do any good. Use that energy to pray and to do what the Lord calls you to do for such a time as this."

"I will, Sweet Charlie, I will," Charlie says softly.

Each of Alphina's letters is meant for Charlie, but he also knows he is not to keep them to himself.

And in this same moment, which stretches out to eternity, Charlie knows the truth. Without a doubt, Charlie knows that the Lord God Almighty does exist. His beloved wife, Pastor Charlie, was right all along. The Creator of the universe, the Great I Am, the Alpha and Omega, the Beginning and the End is alive. And He's in charge.

Charlie, the former math teacher at the local Christian School, falls to his knees and asks the Lord to be the Lord of his life. No longer afraid to pray, Charlie prays with every fiber of his being.

"I surrender to you, O Lord. I surrender my sin, my inaction, my fear, my inadequacies. I ask you to forgive me for not giving up my life for you like my precious Sweet Charlie did. Forgive all my sins, Lord Jesus. Help me to turn away from them for good and to turn toward you. I ask you to lead me and guide me from this moment on, dear Jesus. I give you everything. I am yours now and for eternity. Use me, dear Lord, as weak and inadequate as I am. Use me. I'm your lowly servant. I love you. I praise your holy name. The name above all names! I pray this all in Jesus' name. Amen."

Dear Oliver

PRESENT TIME

Charlie deciphers the newest letter. This one he keeps just for himself.

Dear Oliver,

I think you remember who I am. Maybe not at first, but after I spoke your name out loud to you. Before that you thought that I was just another crazy person locked up for everyone's safety. Oh, I am locked up for safety, but not in the way they think. I'm locked up because the Lord led me here only days before they started hunting Christians. He put me in this place because He has plans for me. Plans that I'm now only starting to realize.

He knows His plans. Plans to prosper us and not to harm us. Plans to give us hope and a future. Oh, that sounds like hogwash to most people now. But you know what I'm saying.

You, my friend, are very much a part of His plan. Did you know that your wife came to visit me here? She came to get me out, but I told her why I had to stay. The Lord called me here. Then suddenly, she knew I was right. And she said she knew she would not live on this earth much longer. She wasn't sad, only in leaving you. She said you would eventually come here, too. That the Lord would use you in mighty ways. She smiled and cried at the same time. She knew it was your calling from the Lord. I hope knowing this gives you peace.

Maybe when I spoke that forbidden, beautiful, life-changing and life-giving name to you, it shocked you into remembering. Remembering who you are. Remembering who you are called to be. Remembering whom you serve. You serve the person behind the forbidden name. You serve Jesus Christ. Don't ever forget that. No matter what happens.

Love,
Alphie

As his Sweet Charlie always said, "There are no coincidences in life, dear Charlie, only God incidents." Her words rang in his heart as an entire network of people living under the radar at BHU begin to act. It's funny how Charlie randomly and continually runs into them. Well, not funny like hilarious, but funny like strange.

God incidents. God working behind the scenes so that they who are not believers don't recognize His hand at work. First, there's Marie. She works in the BHU lunchroom. She helps prepare and serve meals not only for the residents, but also for staff. One day when she sees Charlie going through the line, she smiles at him. She's never done that before.

She looks Charlie directly in the eyes. She's never done that, either. "Charlie, I think you should join our staff card game," she says nonchalantly, saying his name out loud for the very first time.

"It's a simple game called Kings Corner. It helps pass the time for those of us who live here."

Just as Charlie is about to politely decline, he happens to glance up at Marie. She looks at him casually, but there's something insistent in her eyes that will not take "No" for an answer.

152

Then Charlie feels a nudge, like his Sweet Charlie always talked about. "That's the Holy Spirit giving you a suggestion. One you better take. And don't take your time, jump on it!"

"Sounds like a good idea," Charlie says, surprising not only Marie but also himself. Even speaking words out loud to another person is very foreign to Charlie. For just a moment he's transported back to re-education camp where he quickly learns to trust no one and to never speak unless he's told to. And even then, he knows he must be very careful with the words he chooses.

Speak too many words and you just dig yourself a deeper hole that few former Haters ever leave. Speak too few words and those in charge think you're still a Hater, which is by far much, much worse.

Marie clears her throat. To anyone passing by it seems innocent enough, but it also provides an important service. It wakes Charlie out of his remembering and snaps him back to reality.

"Great!" says Marie. "Come back here at 10 o'clock tonight. We'll play at one of the lunchroom tables." Then she turns away and gets back to work. Charlie eats his lunch quickly and goes back to his cleaning, wondering what tonight will hold.

"Is this you leading me, Lord?" he asks, not expecting an answer. Yet, he knows this is exactly what he's supposed to do. Once again, he thinks of Sweet Charlie and smiles. "Yes, dear, I'm listening to the nudgings. Their numbers are increasing and they're becoming more insistent. I'm trying to jump on them!"

Even though he's hesitant and trying his best to be brave, Charlie shows up exactly at 10 p.m. He purposefully looks as if he doesn't care if he's there or not, mindful of a nearby camera.

Marie smiles at him. She looks different in regular clothes without her full-length apron and cap. There's Kyle, the head maintenance man. He and Charlie have exchanged a few words over the years. He's always seemed like a sincere guy.

There's also Fred, the garbage collector, who never seems to be finished with his work. Just like Charlie with his endless cleaning, Fred always finds more garbage to collect, remove, and recycle. In fact, garbage seems to be Fred's mission field.

Charlie can't help but smile at this thought. Sweet Charlie never collected offerings to fund garbage collectors, but maybe she should have. After all, there is a lot of garbage in this world. Even if others see it as valuable, it doesn't make it so. In the end, garbage is still garbage, just like hate is still hate and evil is still evil. No matter how you dress it up, rename it, or sell it on social media, the truth is still the truth.

Charlie recognizes Jim, the groundskeeper. He's an older guy who's still in good shape. He has to be with all the bending, digging, planting, trimming, and weeding he does. He meticulously keeps the grounds looking manicured and pleasant, in a regimented way, of course.

Charlie has thought more than once that when the flowers see Jim coming, they stand straighter, almost as if they're standing at attention.

Nothing grows freely around here. In fact, the word freedom is seldom heard. It hasn't been outlawed, but the concept of freedom has radically changed. Freedom is now what the government tells you freedom is. And you better believe them. It makes life so much easier. It also makes living possible. Anything against the government is lethal.

Last, but not least, there's Sally. She's the secretary to the big boss. Charlie hasn't met her before, which isn't surprising. She works for the important ones in charge. Her position is considered very elite. She must be well trusted. Charlie's a little surprised that she's here. But the elite have special privileges, including free reign of the facility.

Sally is about Charlie's age. She looks at him. There's something about her smile that reminds him of his Sweet

Charlie. Charlie finds this fact surprising, endearing, and a little troublesome. He shakes his head to clear his thoughts. He tells himself to stay in the present and to be careful. Always careful.

"Ready for some cards, everyone?" Marie asks nonchalantly, as she shuffles the deck with the expertise of a Vegas Blackjack dealer.

Each member of the card club takes their place at the table. It's just out of view of the cameras. Still, they all purposefully appear light-hearted, as if there's nothing unusual going on.

Marie smiles at them. "How about some King's Corner?" she asks as she deals the cards. As they go through the motions of playing cards, Charlie looks at each person. He's seen them all around, except for Sally, of course. He realizes they must each have rooms here, too.

"Good old King's Corner," says Kyle. "My brothers and I played this when we were growing up. It's a fun game. We sure had good times back then. Do you know it, Charlie?"

"Sure, I remember, I think." Charlie picks up his cards and puts them in descending order according to suits and color.

It's Sally's turn. She places the King of hearts in a corner. She says, "The King of Hearts is the best card of all."

Charlie thinks this is an odd comment. Is she making up new rules? As far as he knows, the King of Hearts is no different from any other king. It's really no different from any other card, except it's placed in the corner.

Then Kyle says, "I agree. Without the King of Hearts, the other cards wouldn't know what to do. He leads the way."

"I didn't know the King of Hearts until last year. To me, he was just another card. No different from all the rest," says Jim. Charlie notices a little glistening his eyes. Charlie wonders if Jim's getting emotional.

"I know what you mean, Jim. I wasted a lot of years ignoring the King of Hearts, too. All that time I was thinking he was just another card, nothing special. That was until the day I heard

155

him speak to me. Just about lost my mind!" Fred laughs.

"Oh, Fred," Sally says. "You lost your mind long ago." Everyone except Charlie laughs. Charlie is beginning to realize that these people are more than co-workers, they're a family.

Marie smiles at Charlie. Eventually, Charlie, the great code breaker, realizes they're talking in code. Slowly, he realizes the King of Hearts is obviously Jesus Himself.

"Yes, I haven't always appreciated the King of Hearts like I do now," says Charlie. "I, too, wish I hadn't wasted so much time. I didn't know I was so tragically misinformed."

Everyone smiles and looks relieved. They now know they can trust Charlie. They're now certain he's one of them.

The co-workers play several hands. Charlie manages to win the first hand. Marie wins the second one. She ends up winning the most hands. Sally comes in second. But they're really not keeping score as much as communicating with their new believer, Charlie. They're slowly adding to their ragtag army of the Lord.

Before long, others who are Christians hiding in plain sight seek out Charlie. They form a plan of action, always talking in code. A guy delivering bottled water one day, sees Charlie.

"Are you Charlie, the cleaning guy?" he asks.

"I am," Charlie replies cautiously.

"I'm Andrew. I'm the delivery guy. You want anything delivered anywhere at any time, I'm the guy for you."

Charlie keeps mopping the floor. He's about to turn down the hallway when Andrew says, "Yep, I even delivered the King of Hearts to someone just the other day. That was a very special delivery. One I don't often get the privilege to give."

Charlie stops mopping and looks up at Andrew just in time to see him wink. Just as quickly, Andrew turns around and leaves.

You never know who's listening or watching. Even though things are pretty laid back here at the BHU now, everyone must still be very careful and always vigilant. Complacency can be a killer.

Charlie knows this from a few years ago. Martha, another cleaner who lived down the hall from Charlie, was caught with a Bible in her room. She was a quiet, kind woman who never caused any trouble. She went out of her way to be compassionate to all the BHU patients. She never acted like she thought she was better than any of them. In fact, she always took time to greet each one by name.

Martha, well aware that it's illegal to own a Bible, found one hidden under fallen tree branches on the grounds when she was outside taking her daily walk. Without hesitating, she picked it up and hid it under her sweater, going directly to her room.

She opened it to 2 Corinthians 4:6-7. "For God, who said, 'Let there be light in the darkness,' has made this light shine in our hearts so we could know the glory of God that is seen in the face of Jesus Christ. We now have this light shining in our hearts, but we ourselves are like fragile clay jars containing this great treasure. This makes it clear that our great power is from God, not from ourselves."

Martha, enjoying her time with the Word of God, remembered her loving parents and their strong, unshakeable faith. "The Lord's light shined through them," she thought. "They lived out their faith every day of their lives."

Martha sighed, missing her mom and dad. "They knew where their power came from. That's how they could stand together holding hands in front of the firing squad." Martha remembered seeing them on TV. Labeled Haters, they didn't survive the week after the President signed the Anti-Hate Law.

"Where did I go wrong?" Martha asked herself. She didn't have to go to re-education camp. She readily accepted the fact that the Haters needed to be stopped. She knew, of course, that she wasn't one of them and she told anyone who would listen. The authorities easily believed her. She certainly didn't live like a believer.

But now she asked herself again, "Where did I go wrong?" She knew the answer. It started in college when she questioned everything she'd ever been taught. It's natural to want to be independent, but Martha knew she took it too far. Every liberal idea she bumped into, stuck to her and penetrated her soul like a cancer. When all her friends decided that God was just a fairytale, Martha joined in their storyline. She could repeat it almost word for word. Her parents tried to steer her back to the Lord, but she was rigidly stubborn. It's one of her biggest regrets.

"Lord, I am a fragile clay jar. So breakable. So fragile. You are the one with all the power. Help me to return to you, Jesus. Give me real faith, like my parents had. Please, dear Jesus."

In that moment, time slowed down, and Martha felt the power of the Holy Spirit in her. She felt His presence all around her. She knew that no matter what happened from now on, His light was shining in her. And she knew she would be okay. Peace invaded her and filled up all her empty spaces.

Martha enjoyed reading God's Word every chance she got. One night she was reading it when the Peacekeepers broke into her room and grabbed the Bible. They burned her Bible on the front lawn for all to see. Martha was taken to the interrogation room. She was never seen again.

Charlie was cleaning outside the interrogation room knowing that Martha was inside. He heard no sounds coming from the room, but he saw a light shining through the cracks in the door. He recognized that light from when his Sweet Charlie spoke the name above all names in the courtroom. The name of Jesus. And when she was assassinated, he saw the light surround her and shoot up toward the ceiling and out of the building. The very Light of God shining in the darkness and through one of His own.

Charlie

PRESENT TIME

During one card game night, Charlie manages to convey the fact that he has access to inspirational words about the King of Hearts. "I think the King of Hearts would like these words to be distributed to others."

The others catch on to what Charlie is carefully saying. He has letters written in code that he can decipher. They should be taken to other believers in hiding as a way of encouraging them. A way to show them that they are not alone. A way to give hope to the remnant in hiding.

Slowly, the King of Hearts players handwrite Alphina's letters. They distribute them to those they know are in hiding. How do they know? Some they've met by chance. Others, the Lord leads them to.

Charlie with the photographic memory knows where May and the others he met on that fateful day are hiding. Pretty much all the memories he lost in the re-education camp have now returned. In fact, his mind is sharper than it's ever been.

"I'm sure the Lord has a part in this," thinks Charlie. "Without His help, I wouldn't remember anything from before, but now I seem to remember all the befores. Before the day the garage door opened. Before the day it became a federal offense to believe in God. Before anyone ever heard of the re-education camps that were hiding throughout this country like scavengers waiting for their prey."

Charlie remembers his Sweet Charlie telling him about believers in third world countries where Christianity was traditionally more than frowned upon. Christians were persecuted and sometimes even tortured and killed.

"They have to meet in underground churches, Charlie. They have to gather in secret to worship the Lord together. Can you imagine that?"

No, of course, Charlie couldn't imagine that back then. In the first place, he's never been known for a great imagination. In the second place, he's the numbers guy. It's who he is. He likes, and once simply expected, life to be predictable. To add up as easily as numbers written in chalk on an elementary school blackboard.

But now Charlie can imagine what life must have been like for those in the underground churches. Those moving stealthily around like mice secretly living in a house. Hiding at every unknown sound. Scurrying around every corner. Hoping for a little morsel of something to eat.

Whereas mice are looking for food, Charlie and others are searching for the food of God. The Word Himself. "In the beginning was the Word and the Word was with God and the Word was God."

And not only for themselves, but to share with others.

He also remembers something else his Sweet Charlie said. "When believers live under that kind of persecution, their faith becomes amazingly strong. They see and experience things we simply don't. They see God working in miraculous ways. There are so many stories of the blind being healed and the lame made to walk. Of persecutors being thwarted. Of persecutors becoming believers. It's amazing! When we trust Him with everything, God shows up big ways. In ways that even those with the greatest imaginations can never imagine."

At the time, Charlie listened to his Sweet Charlie, but he didn't really know what she was talking about. But now, oh now he knows. He's part of a very secret and very dangerous team of believers living in a country and a world that not only blatantly and proudly hates Christians, they demand that everyone else hates them, too.

Yet, despite everything that's happened and is happening, this little ragtag card group follows the King of Hearts. They are bringing the Lord's hope to God's remnant, which is much larger than anyone suspects.

Funny that Charlie's full name is Charlie Oliver Pasture. His initials are C.O.P. and he's breaking every law there is. If he's caught, his sentence will be swift, and it will be without mercy.

Just like the numbers he loves so much; he knows what danger plus danger equals. Death. But he doesn't worry about that anymore. In fact, the numbers guy spends every waking hour devising ways to add others to the Lord's flock before his time on this earth is over.

The Dear Oliver letters are a big part of that. In fact, in this postmodern era, it's funny to think that old fashioned, handwritten letters are the tools used to encourage the remnant, the believers in hiding. And they may even add more people to the flock before the Good Shepherd returns for His people.

Ray and Molly

PRESENT TIME

May and the other adults recognize that the children need some fresh air. They pray first, of course, as they always do. Then they take the kids outside on a regular basis. One day Molly, Ray, Pearl, Daisy, and Kate take Beth, Erin and Jonah outdoors. They stay within the inner grove of trees. It's a natural sanctuary. They feel safe here. And it smells so nice. Like being surrounded by hundreds of those scented Christmas trees from long ago. The kind that you could hang from your car's rearview mirror. Every time you opened the door it smelled like Christmas.

Thankfully, the sunlight is bright today and everyone's mood lifts as they feel the warmth on their faces as they breathe in the fresh air.

Beth and Erin immediately start a game of tag. The two moms, along with Molly and Ray, join in. Pearl watches and laughs at their antics. Ray is by far the slowest one, but he also seems to be enjoying it the most.

Molly loves the sound of her husband's laughter. It takes her back to when they were first married, and he joked all the time. But life eventually got harder and there were many disappointments. With every setback, Ray's laughter became less and less, until one day Molly realized that Ray never seemed to laugh anymore.

That's the day Molly prayed for Ray's laughter to return. She also prayed to be the best wife she could be. She asked the Lord to show her ways to help Ray and to truly be his helpmate.

Molly has always loved her Ray. From the minute she saw him on the football field in high school, she knew she would someday marry him. They've had a good life together, but ever since he gave his heart to the Lord, Ray's a changed man. He's the same but so much more. He's more loving and more kind. He speaks more with everyone, not just her. He appreciates everything, but he especially loves the children. And they have taken to him as a beloved uncle.

God not only answered Molly's prayers, He went above and beyond what she asked for. Throughout her life, Molly has found this to be true. That's why she has so much to be thankful for. A lifelong believer, Molly is a rare Christian in that she has never questioned the Lord. Not even once.

And Molly doesn't remember a time when she wasn't following Him. She doesn't remember a time when He didn't hear her prayers and eventually answer them. Not as she always wanted, of course. But the Lord has always given her what she's truly needed. She is so thankful. It's no wonder she leads a life of thanksgiving. It doesn't take long for those around her to see the calm, grateful way in which she lives. She's an inspiration without realizing it.

Thankfully, since they are in such an isolated place, there are no sounds of any motors going by. It isn't one of the days when drones come around. And there's a peacefulness in the air.

But Pearl senses that something is wrong. She learned long ago to pay attention to this feeling. Once when her husband Elmer came home in the middle of a terrible ice storm, he parked not far from the house. Immediately, Pearl knew that something was terribly wrong. She ran outside in the cold and pelting ice. "Move your car, Elmer! Move your car forward! Now!" she yelled at her husband.

Elmer didn't hesitate. He immediately ran back to his car, quickly hopped in and moved it about 100 feet forward. Just as he was getting out of his car, the sound of something cracking filled the air. A 300-pound tree limb broke off and landed on a power line directly above where Elmer's car sat just minutes before.

Looking at Pearl, Elmer once again knew that the Lord spoke to her. As the limb crashed to the ground and took out their power, he thanked the Lord for not only his safety, but also for his wife and her unshakeable faith.

All these years later, Pearl knows something is terribly wrong. She asks the Lord what it is. She looks up and sees Jonah high up in one of the trees. She knows he's in imminent danger.

Pearl says, without alarm, "You better come down from there, Jonah." The others stop what they're doing. They look up in time to see Jonah wave. As he waves, he loses his balance and falls to the ground. Oddly, his fall seems to be in slow motion. His mom, Daisy, is the first one to get to him.

"He's not breathing," she yells. The others inside the house are now here. Heather leans down next to Jonah. She looks him over quickly and then begins CPR. She starts the chest compressions. Thirty of them. Next she tilts Jonah's head back. She pinches his nose shut and breathes two breaths into his mouth. She watches as his chest rises and then lowers. She repeats this pattern over and over.

May and Frank hold hands and pray. The others join them, except for Pearl and Daisy. Daisy is still on the ground next to Jonah, sobbing her prayers. Heather is still administering CPR. It isn't working. Heather is exhausted, but she won't give up. She knows it's Jonah's only hope. Everyone is counting on her. She feels the pressure to perform.

Just like when Heather was a little girl, her perfectionistic parents made her do everything over and over again until it was perfect. Of course, the more she strived for perfection, the farther away it became. When she thinks about her life growing up, the main thing she remembers is that her parents were always disappointed in her.

To this day Heather is still nervous around people who remind her of her mom and dad. She loved them and they loved her, but no matter what she did, she never quite measured up.

Heather keeps going. Thirty compressions, two breaths. Thirty, two. Thirty, two. Thirty. Two.

Pearl kneels on the ground and touches Heather's arm gently. "Let me try," she says. Surprised, Heather moves aside.

Pearl leans over Jonah and places her hands onto his face. Then she moves them under his head, almost cradling it. She closes her eyes and says quietly, "Lord of all creation, we know nothing is impossible for you. We humbly ask you to place your healing touch on our precious Jonah. Just like you miraculously brought Jonah out of the big fish's belly so long ago, bring our Jonah out of death's door and back to the land of the living. We need him, Lord. He is part of the next generation of believers. We pray this in Jesus' name. Amen."

"What do we do now?" asks Daisy.

"We wait," says Pearl. "We wait to see if the Lord decides to heal Jonah on earth or in heaven."

Daisy breaks into sobs. Heather puts her arms around her. Daisy cries all the tears she has, then she cries some more. "Where is Jim? Why isn't he here with me? What's happened to him?" Daisy speaks out loud all the thoughts she hasn't even allowed herself to think.

"Is he still alive?" She cries some more. In fact, her swollen eyes become black and blue from all the crying.

As she cries, Daisy remembers Jonah's birth. It was so easy that she told Jim that it was like a stroll in the park. A smile turns at the corner of Daisy's mouth. She thinks to herself, "Ever since the day he was born, Jonah has been an easy child. Kind and caring, he's been a joy to raise."

Daisy silently prays, "Lord, Jonah is such a good boy. You know him well. Please heal him. Please. Please."

Then there is total silence, as if everyone present is holding their collective breath. And not only the people, but nature itself. No wind. No birds chirping. No rustling of leaves. No sound at all.

Suddenly, a loud gasp invades the silence. It's the sound of Jonah taking a way-down deep breath.

"A whale of a breath," thinks Heather.

Jonah's chest rises and lowers. Rises and lowers. Finally, Jonah opens his eyes and says, "What's everyone looking at?"

The roommates laugh except for Daisy who grabs her Jonah and hugs him tightly. "Thank you! Thank you!" she says to Pearl.

"Don't thank me," says Pearl. "Thank the Lord! He's the one who performs miracles, not me."

Everyone joins in thanking the Lord for this precious miracle. There's a chorus of praises going directly to the throne room of God. Such a sweet sound. Such a lovely aroma of celebration.

Ray, who's blubbering, is the loudest one of all. "Thank you, Jesus! Thank you for saving our Jonah! I'm sorry that I ever doubted you! Forgive me, Lord!"

Oh, the resiliency of youth. Jonah wants to jump right up, but Daisy says, "Just rest for a minute, Jonah. Let's make sure you're okay. That was quite a fall."

"It didn't hurt," says Jonah. Everyone looks at him with surprise on their faces and questions in their minds.

"The fall. It didn't hurt at all. All the time I was falling, time just slowed way down. I could see you all looking at me. I could feel the wind on my face, but it was blowing in slow motion. I wasn't afraid.

"Then I felt these big, strong arms holding me. When I hit the ground, it didn't hurt at all. It was like landing on a giant pillow. I wanted to laugh, but I couldn't.

"Then I saw you all standing around me. I felt Heather breathing for me. I heard Pearl praying for me. And you, too, Mom. Even though you were praying silently, I could hear your words." Daisy nods.

"And everyone else, too. Ray, I heard your prayers, too."

"But mine were silent," says Ray.

"God hears them all," Jonah says. "And guess what? They smell nice. Sweet. Like all the prayers were going straight up to God. And I knew in that moment that whether the Lord healed me on earth or healed me in heaven that I would be okay."

Everyone is still. They're all taking in Jonah's words that seem to be coming from someone much, much older. They're mulling over and savoring this miracle from God Himself.

And each person in this make-shift family knows the truth. Whether God intervenes in this crazy world and sets things straight now, or waits until they all get to heaven, they will be all right.

"Surely the presence of the Lord is in this place," says Pearl. "And He knows we need Jonah here with us. Thank you, Lord!"

Pearl begins singing, "All hail the power of Jesus' name! Let angels prostrate fall. Bring forth the royal diadem and crown him Lord of all. Bring forth the royal diadem and crown him Lord of all!"

The others join in praising God for His mercy and His goodness. They break into their own familiar hymns and songs. It could sound like a cacophony of noise, but somehow Pearl knows that their praise singing is going straight to the throne room of the Almighty and that He loves the sound.

Kate, Erin and Beth

PRESENT TIME

Everyone gathers in the living room where they have daily devotions together. Today, Pearl reads from the book of Judges in chapter six about Gideon.

"Then the children of Israel did evil in the sight of the LORD. So the LORD delivered them into the hand of Midian for seven years, and the hand of Midian prevailed against Israel. Because of the Midianites, the children of Israel made for themselves the dens, the caves, and the strongholds which are in the mountains."

Erin speaks up. "So, they went into hiding just like we're doing."

"I'm so thankful we don't have to live in a cave. Bats live there!" says Beth as she makes a funny face.

Mom Kate chuckles. "As a family, we once went on a cave tour. It was fun until the bats showed up."

Erin continues, "They were everywhere! We all ran around in circles screaming."

"Even Daddy," says Beth. At the mention of his name, Beth's eyes fill with tears. "I wonder how he is," she says in a tiny voice. Erin takes her hand and holds it tightly.

"God is watching out for him," says Kate.

"Do you think he's scared?" asks Erin.

"He's a smart man," says Kate. "I'm sure he's scared, but he knows there's someone bigger than all of us watching out for him."

"Jesus." Erin and Beth say at the same time. The others nod, knowing it's true, but still harboring some fear. The large living room is quiet as each person is lost in their own thoughts, thinking of loved ones not with them. Especially those who were alive during and after Liberation Day.

Pearl continues her Bible reading. "Now the Angel of the LORD came and sat under the terebinth tree which was in Ophrah, which belonged to Joash the Abiezrite, while his son Gideon threshed wheat in the winepress, in order to hide it from the Midianites. And the Angel of the LORD appeared to him, and said to him, 'The LORD is with you, you mighty man of valor!'"

"Mighty man of valor, what does that mean?" asks Jonah.

"It means someone who is courageous even though the odds seem stacked against him. Someone who follows the Lord even though he may lose his life," Pearl says.

"Was that Gideon?" Asks Jonah.

Pearl laughs. "It sure doesn't seem like it at this moment. He's threshing wheat where he can't be seen. He's hiding, really. Later he says he's the least in all his family. He doubts that he can do anything at all. But the Lord calls him to deliver Israel from Midian. Here, let me read a little more."

"Gideon said to Him, 'O my lord, if the LORD is with us, why then has all this happened to us? And where are all His miracles which our fathers told us about, saying, 'Did not the LORD bring us up from Egypt?' But now the LORD has forsaken us and delivered us into the hands of the Midianites."

"I'm surprised that Gideon questions God," says Erin.

"That's just who we human beings are, Honey," Molly says,

laughing one of her big laughs. "We're not so different from Gideon. We question the Lord because we're afraid and we don't believe down deep that He'll really help us."

"That's right," says Kate. "As long as everything is going the way we want it to go, we are happily faithful. We might even have a little bit of pride about the way we're following the Lord. But it doesn't take any real faith or courage to follow God in the easy times."

"Remember what Daddy always says?" asks Beth. "'Amateur Christians follow the Lord when everything is easy but run away during the first sign of trouble.'"

"Your dad sounds like a wise man," says Pearl. Beth nods her head up and down.

Pearl continues. "Then the LORD turned to him and said, 'Go in this might of yours, and you shall save Israel from the hand of the Midianites. Have I not sent you?' So he said to Him, 'O my Lord, how can I save Israel? Indeed my clan is the weakest in Manasseh, and I am the least in my father's house.'"

"He's making excuses, isn't he?" asks Erin.

"Yes," says Pearl. "Does that sound familiar? We all make excuses at times when we don't think we can do what God asks us to do."

"But we don't do it anyhow," says Erin. "It's the Lord who does it."

Pearl smiles at Erin. "You're so right. You're a smart girl." She continues reading. "And the LORD said to him, 'Surely I will be with you, and you shall defeat the Midianites as one man.'"

"You see, Honey," says Molly. "God doesn't choose us because of who we are. He chooses us because of who He is. Gideon isn't a mighty man of valor. He's just like you and me. Afraid of the unknown. Afraid of a mighty enemy. But Gideon believes in God. And God uses that tiny bit of faith and then He makes Gideon into a mighty warrior. He calls Gideon and then He equips him."

171

Suddenly, May, who's been quiet this whole time speaks up. "I think I understand. I don't know why it took me so long!"

"What?" asks Frank.

"What?" asks Ray, who's learning so far forward to listen, Molly's afraid he'll topple over.

May looks at each person present. Her gaze stays on Frank. "We're not in hiding. We're in waiting. We're waiting for the Lord to call us just like He called Gideon. And we don't have to be afraid. He's with us. He's called us. He'll equip us, when the time is right."

Later that day, Jonah ventures outside and sees something under the rock. It's the first time that he's spotted one of the letters. He grabs it and runs inside. "It's here! It's here! Another Dear Oliver Letter! It's here!"

From all nooks and crannies in the house, the roommates come running. They nod at one another as they head for the living room. By now they have their favorite spots. Each one gets comfortable in their spot.

Jonah offers May the letter. "Jonah, I think you should read it," she says. Maybe there's a reason that you're the one who found it.

"Really?" he asks, surprised. "Okay, I will." Jonah gets comfortable and looks over at his mom. She smiles and nods as if to say, "Go ahead."

Dear Oliver,

Things are moving along very well now. I know what you are all doing. You're like postal workers without getting paid. But as you all already know, this is more about life than making a living. It's more about eternal life than life here on earth. Don't give up. Keep going. The Lord has called you. He's equipping you. He's with you every step of the way.

Remember the old postal saying? I'm not sure if I remember it correctly, but here it goes: "Neither snow, nor rain, nor heat, nor dark of night stays these couriers from the swift completion of their appointed rounds."

You all have your appointed rounds. The Lord Himself has called you. He knows who needs to hear from other believers. He knows who's in hiding, waiting for Him to tell them what to do. Whether He calls them to stay where they are or to move on, He'll tell them. Maybe He'll ask them to stay put until He comes back to take His beloved church home. We don't know. But thankfully we love and serve the One who does. Never forget that.

And never stop praying for those who are squirreled away throughout this country not knowing what will happen next. Many don't know what has happened to their loved ones who aren't with them. That's where faith comes in. We must have faith knowing that the Lord knows where they are. Just as He's watching out for us, He's watching out for them.

Remember Gideon?

Jonah stops reading and looks at everyone in the room. "How does she know that we were just talking about Gideon?"

"She doesn't know," says Erin. "But God does." Jonah goes back to reading.

Remember Gideon? The Mighty Man of Valor. He wasn't a mighty man of anything except hiding on the threshing floor. But when God got a hold of him and called him, he became who God said he was, a mighty man of valor.

May we all become exactly who the Lord calls us to be. He knows who we are. And He knows who we will be if we follow Him. We must continue to follow Him. He has called us to live in this time, in this country, and for such a time as this. He's already equipping each one of us for battle. My sword is the words He gives me. Your sword is something entirely different. With a little faith, the Lord makes each one of us men and women, and boys and girls of valor.

Love, Alphie

Charlie

PRESENT TIME

Charlie deciphers a new letter from Alphie. He still has a hard time believing that no one in authority has figured out what he's doing. "Thank you, Lord, for protecting me," Charlie says under his breath. "Not only for myself, but also for those you want to read these words. Continue to lead me and guide me, Lord. Amen."

Dear Oliver,
By now you know who I am and who I was, in our other life. The life before the world became insane. I know, it's funny for an inmate in the BHU to talk about the sanity of others. You have my permission to laugh.
I don't know why, but lately memories come flooding into my mind and I have to wade through them to get to the nearby shore. Here's one that came to me today.
I can still see the picture on the wall in my grandparents' living room, even though it hasn't hung there for decades. It was right next to my grandfather's favorite chair. The one that sat directly in front of the TV.

175

The picture is in a big, beautiful oval oak frame with beveled glass. Two young children are holding hands. They're standing on the edge of a cliff. The weather is threatening. A big storm is brewing, but the children are unaware of the pending danger.

The boy is standing in front of the girl. He's wearing a white shirt. He reaches behind himself with one hand to hold the girl's hand. She's wearing a red skirt and a white blouse. She's bending over picking wildflowers.

The boy's other hand reaches out in front of him, out past the safety of the ground. He's straining to catch a butterfly in flight. Neither child looks afraid. They seem unaware that what they're doing is dangerous. They're in this together.

Behind them, is a tall guardian angel. Even from the world of the painting, her mighty power and strength are evident and awe-inspiring. She stands directly behind the children with her arms outstretched in a protective manner. The boy and the girl don't know the angel is there, but she's there, nonetheless, calmly watching over them.

Do they somehow sense the angel's presence? Do they somehow hear the unspoken words, "Fear not?" How are they able to be out in a brewing storm, reaching over a cliff and not look afraid?

I remember a particular time in my life when I was searching. Not for butterflies, although I did that a lot when I was a little girl. But searching for my place in this world. Wondering what God was calling me to do. Asking what my purpose was. Wondering if God could use me in any way like He used people in the Bible. After all, those people were just ordinary people like me. I had a feeling of unrest. As if I was supposed to be doing more, but I didn't know what the "more" was.

Mixed up in all of this was a little bit of fear. What if God never answered my prayer? What if I said, "Send me," but He never asked me to go anywhere? What if I simply lived my life out here on earth never really doing anything? I was vague on

176

what the something in that anything should be, but I sensed I was called for more. For something. But what if I never figured it out?

Then one night I had a dream. I was standing on the very edge of a cliff. A huge storm was brewing. The dark clouds were rolling in at amazing speed. The air was charged with threatening possibilities, but I stood on the very edge of that cliff completely unafraid. My arms were outstretched in front of me, in a receiving stance. I was waiting. Not for the storm. I ignored the storm. I was waiting for something else. The storm raged all around me. Still, I wasn't afraid.

Then I saw Him. I saw Jesus in the midst of the storm. He was larger than life itself. Quietly powerful, He wasn't simply surrounded by peace, He was the very essence of peace. And He looked right at me. He saw me. He knew me. He hugged me. He loved me. Peace and joy and love flooded me. I no longer saw the storm. I only saw the One who calms the storms. Seeing Him calmed the storms in me.

Somewhere in that dream I decided to give up worrying about what to do with my life and I simply followed Him. I knew that He'd take me where He wanted me to go. And I knew without a doubt that He'd go with me.

And He has. He does. Every day. Every step. My job is to try to keep up. My job is to mirror the love He gives me. Maybe that's why I like storms. Because in the center of them, I always find Jesus.

We're in the midst of the biggest storm we've ever encountered. It sounds trite, but it's true. We are in the Battle of Good versus Evil. It's an age-old battle that began in heaven when Lucifer the angel rebelled against God. He wanted to be God, but only God can be God.

The battle continued in the Garden of Eden when Satan tempted Eve. Both Eve and Adam sinned. Sin has continued for all these many generations. Thankfully, the Father loves us so much that He sent His Son, Jesus, to earth not to condemn

177

us but to save us from our sins.

In the midst of this tumultuous battle, we have the advantage. We know who wins in the end. And we know who is with us every step of the way. Our Lord and Savior, Jesus Christ. Let's never forget that. Never forget.

Love, Alphie

Never forget. Charlie will never forget. He'll never forget his Sweet Charlie, the love of his life. The Charlie with the strong faith. They had such a wonderful marriage, but it could have been even better if he'd only truly given his life to the Lord while she was alive. He thought he believed, but as he discovered through all of this, he was riding on his wife's faith, thinking it would get him into heaven, too. He regrets the years he wasted not truly following the Lord. He regrets the time that could have been even sweeter if he'd been the true spiritual leader of their family.

But there's no time for regret now. Charlie's too busy pretending to be who the authorities want him to be as he stealthily does the Lord's work. Why just today he deciphered five more letters and carefully delivered them to Marie in the lunchroom.

"She would have made an expert spy," Charlie chuckles to himself. "She's pretty sneaky. And Sweet Charlie would have liked her," Charlie thinks to himself. "That's for sure. Two peas in a pod. Oh, not the sneaky part, but the creative part and the unshakeable faith. Well, they're also both born leaders."

Charlie doesn't think it odd at all that he has entire conversations with himself. He's basically been alone since re-education camp. He's been afraid to talk too much with others. He's been too afraid to trust anyone.

But all that has changed. Many of his conversations recently are with the Lord. After all, He's the one who's leading and guiding Charlie now. No longer a slave to fear, doubt, and regret, Charlie shines with God's love. Even some of the residents on the BHU floors have noticed.

One lady recently asked, "What have you been doing with yourself, Charlie? You look different. You look good."

Charlie just smiles and keeps cleaning. Another lady said, "Charlie, you're getting more handsome every day!"

Charlie doesn't tell them it's the Lord's love that has changed him, even though he wants to. He wants to shout it from the rooftop. "Jesus is my Lord and He has changed my life!" But he doesn't. Not because he's afraid. Strangely, he's not afraid at all. He doesn't shout it because he knows that his work would be finished. "And my time hasn't come yet," thinks Charlie. "I don't know how I know, but I do. My work is just beginning."

Alphina and the New Doc

PRESENT TIME

"Hi Alphina," says a doctor at the BHU after he knocks on her door and enters. "I'm Dr. Michael. I'm new here at the BHU and I hear you've been here a very long time."

She smiles a sweet smile but says nothing understandable, except the following numbers: "8, 9 (pause) 4,15, 3." (Hi Doc.)

"That's okay," I've heard that you don't speak, at least not in words." He walks around the room and pauses, looking at the typewritten pages taped on the wall. After Charlie the Cleaner took them down, it wasn't long before Alphina typed up more and taped them to the walls. The workers in the BHU think it's funny how busy Charlie is inspecting Alphina's room and removing the latest gibberish.

"But I have heard that at times you speak in numbers," continues Dr. Michael. "I find that fascinating, Miss Alphina. You see, when I was a little boy my best friend and I loved math. In fact, we'd sometimes talk in numbers. We even made up our own language. The funny part is that no one else ever caught on. It was our secret language."

Dr. Michael stops speaking and looks directly at Alphina.

He smiles a kind smile and then he speaks again. He says, "8, 9 (pause) 1, 12, 16, 8, 9, 14, 1." (Hi Alphina.)

Alphina almost falls off her chair. Dr. Michael knows her secret! He knows the code! Panic fills her soul and takes up residence on her face.

"It's okay, it's okay," Dr. Michael says soothingly, as if he's speaking to a small child. "I'm here to help. The One who shines in the darkness has sent me to you." Alphina visibly calms down. "For such a time as this." Alphina smiles.

Dr. Michael walks around Alphina's room again. He stops and reads more of the typewritten pages taped to the wall. He easily deciphers them as if he's bilingual and simply reading another language in which he's fluent.

He looks at the elderly BHU patient with love. "I agree, Miss Alphina. Our world has turned upside down and inside out, but He is still in charge. And He has sent me to help you. Will you let me?"

Then Dr. Michael points to himself and says, "3, 8, 18, 9, 19, 20, 9, 1, 14," (Christian).

Alphina, relieved, smiles at Dr. Michael and says, "2, 18, 15, 20, 8, 5, 18" (Brother).

Dr. Michael becomes a regular visitor to Alphina's room. The other professionals are amazed at his patience. "He must be a saint," one of the doctors comments to his nurse. The nurse responds, "Yes, he must be."

Neither of them sees the irony of referring to anyone in religious terms, especially now. But Dr. Michael is a saint. Oh, not in the sense that he's canonized. He's not. But in the sense that saint means "set aside." Dr. Michael is set aside for the Lord's work.

Frank and Jonah

CHRISTMAS DAY

It's hard to believe it's Christmas Day at the farm today. So much has happened in the last few months.

Even though this makeshift family is hidden in the country, and they don't have access to stores or even to other people, each member has planned something special for this big day. There's definitely an air of excitement as each one greets the sunrise on Christmas Day.

Frank wakes up filled with peace and hope. He rushes downstairs to meet with Jonah, as they planned the night before. They're going outside today for just a short time. Jonah has a surprise in mind for his mom.

They pray together, then go outdoors. Jonah found some red ribbon the day before that May said he could have. He has it with him now. The two search around the evergreen trees.

"Here it is," says Frank. They look at the foot of an especially large tree. Fallen branches line the ground.

"These will work perfectly!" Jonah says excitedly.

"Let's pick them up and take them inside. Maybe Molly will

let us put it together in the basement."

"I know she will!" says Jonah.

As they finish up, it begins to snow heavily. The trees and ground quickly turn white. The snowflakes are unusually large. Jonah sticks out his tongue, trying to catch some. Frank laughs and does the same. If they didn't know better, someone watching this scene would think that a father and his son were outside playing together.

"Frank, everything looks so clean, doesn't it?" asks Jonah. "Like the outdoors is getting ready to celebrate Christmas, too."

"I couldn't have said it better myself, Jonah," says Frank.

Of course, May has been up for a long time. Her Harry once showed her how to bake bread without electricity. "You'll need to know this one day, May Day."

May stopped asking Harry why he was always saying things like this. She slowly came to realize that the Lord gave Harry discernment and knowledge for future times.

Oh, there were little things at first. Like the time May was carrying a huge pot of boiling water filled with cooked spaghetti noodles over to the sink. Harry warned her, "Be careful, May." Before he finished speaking, May slipped and the boiling water leaped out of the pot onto May's right foot. "Oh!" is all that she could say.

Harry immediately began praying. When May reached down to touch her sandaled foot, it wasn't harmed. It was covered in water. The leather strap going across her foot was wet and very warm, but her foot was unharmed.

"My foot. My foot, Harry," stammered May. "It's okay."

"Praise the Lord!" Harry said with great thanks and praise.

May came to accept what Harry said would happen someday as true. And she vowed to remember all that her husband shared with her. In fact, that became a daily part of her prayers. "Lord, help me to remember all that I need to know."

"Now listen, May Day," says Harry. "When I'm gone and

you eventually move to town, leave everything behind that you don't need. Leave it right here in our house. Lock the doors and walk away. The Lord will protect this place. He always has and He always will. It's been our sanctuary and one day it will be a sanctuary for you and for others. And on that day, when I'm long gone, you'll be thankful for this place all over again."

May remembers Harry smiling because he knew the truth. May was thankful for this old house. To her it was a mansion because it's where she lived with her Harry. And they were happy in their simple life together out in the country in the middle of nowhere Nebraska in this humble house where the Lord resides.

Once again, Harry knew what he was talking about. More and more May realizes that the Lord was truly using Harry long ago to help May and the others survive today's crazy world.

May tries making the bread today and it works. Using a cookie pan lined with tea candles, she places a metal cooling rack on top. Then she mixes up the ingredients for bread and leaves them to rise. After the dough has risen, she lights the candles and places the bread bowl in another bowl and places them on the cooling rack.

The smell of baking bread fills the farmhouse, reminding her of Harry who always said, "May Day, this place smells like heaven!"

"Yes, Lord," thinks May. "Today this home smells like heaven because You are here with us. Thank you! And thank you, Lord, for being with us today and every day. You truly are our Bread of Life, fulfilling all our needs. Just like when the people of Israel left Egypt, you are with us in this wilderness. Today we celebrate the birth of your Son and the many gifts you give us, including this manna of fresh baked bread. Amen."

Dear Oliver

CHRISTMAS DAY

Dear Oliver,
I love this new doctor, Dr. Michael. Have you met him yet?
He's kind. He's funny. And best of all, he's one of us. He truly
is. If I didn't know better, I'd think he was an angel sent from
God. Just like the archangel Michael in the Bible, he fights for
God's people. We can trust him.
And he knows me so well. He even speaks my language.
Our language.
He's pretending to help me in a clinical way so that those
in charge won't get suspicious of all the time he spends with
me. And he is helping me, in so many ways.
I know he's a gift from God for such a time as this. He's
like the son I never had. I have both a motherly and a sisterly
love for him. I pray for him daily. Well, several times a day. I'm
taking Apostle Paul's words, "Pray continually," seriously.
Dr. Michael has been a believer since he was very young.
His childhood friend was a Christian and somehow gave his
life for Michael. I'm sure that one day he'll share the whole

story with me. I know it's a powerful one. I feel it in my very soul. That Bible verse pops into my mind each time I see him. "Greater love has no one than to give his life for a friend."

It was after his childhood friend, Timothy, died that Dr. Michael gave his life to the Lord. He vowed to serve Him the rest of his life. I know this is risky, but I felt a nudge from the Holy Spirit, so I told Dr. Michael about you. Don't be surprised if he approaches you. He'll help us in any way he can.

And yes, he has read all the letters since he's been here. I know he'll read this one the next time he visits if you don't pick it up before he comes. God is working all around us. He's on the move through people like you and Dr. Michael. Both of you are gifts to me as I celebrate Christmas today by thanking God for you.

Our Savior humbled Himself to come to this earth in the form of a helpless baby. He came into this dark world to spread His Light of love to all who choose to follow Him. In honor of Him, I wrote a Christmas poem today. I want to share it with you. It's called, Christmas Lullaby.

Christmas Lullaby
Don't hush the little baby. He won't cry. He wrote his very own lullaby. It's a song of peace. It's a song of love, as beautiful as the angels singing praises above.

It starts at the beginning, but it has no end. This baby knows that one day he's coming back again. He was with the Father when the world began. Both Light and darkness took a stand.

Don't wait too long before you join His side. Lay down your stubbornness. Lay down your pride. Look at the shadow across the baby's bed. The cross starts at His toes and covers his head. But don't worry or fret or be afraid. The baby is the Way – from death to eternal life in Heaven one day.

So, join in this sweet baby's lullaby. He gives us joy. He makes us cry. His love is the sweetest sound you'll ever hear

— *today, tomorrow, and forever and a year.*

I share this today for you, my dear friend, my brother Oliver. May God bless you, protect you, and keep you until He comes to take you home to be with Him in glory. Merry Christmas!

Love, Alphina

Pearl

CHRISTMAS DAY

Pearl wakes up early Christmas Day. She's thankful for this new family to call her own. She never admitted it before, but she was lonely living by herself. She didn't realize it until now. She missed having others to care about.

She has a special surprise for each one today. But first, she follows her nose to the kitchen. "What is that heavenly smell?" Pearl asks.

"Well, it's an experiment. Bread in a pot," laughs May. "I hope it works. My husband, Harry, showed me how to make it years ago. He said I'd need to know one day."

Pearl nods her head in agreement as if she knows what Harry was talking about. "I guess he was right. I've come to believe, Pearl, that the Lord gave Harry knowledge way back then to help us right now."

"I believe that's true, May. He does that for us. It's one of the many ways He helps us."

The two women smile at one another knowing that they are sisters in the Lord. "Oh, I almost forgot!" says May. "I have something for you, Pearl. It's something my Harry gave me long ago and I know that he'd want you to have it."

May opens a drawer and carefully removes a box. "This is for you." May hands it to Pearl. Pearl opens it. She doesn't speak for a few minutes. Then a tear slides down her cheek.

"Oh, May. This is lovely. A set of pink pearls with a small cross in the front. Pink is my favorite color. The cross makes me think of the Lord and His sacrifice for me. And you know how I feel about pearls." They both laugh then hug.

"But are you sure you want to give this to me? It's from your Harry."

"Yes, Pearl. Nothing gives me more joy than to give you a gift from Harry. I know that he would have treasured you, just as I do."

"Thank you, May. Thank you!" says Pearl.

Charlie

CHRISTMAS DAY

Charlie smiles as he cleans the hallway. It hasn't been that long, but his life has changed dramatically in the last few months. He truly knows the joy his Sweet Charlie had. He's thankful for her example. He's thankful for the seeds of true faith her life planted in him.

Charlie is thankful for Alphie, too. For her faith, for her memories of Sweet Charlie, and for her letters. Charlie's thankful for his card group. They call themselves The King of Hearts because that's who they serve.

But most of all, Charlie's thankful that the Lord has truly forgiven him of his sins. Charlie knows without a doubt that he's a part of the Lord's family today. And for the very first time in his life, he feels clean. Charlie chuckles at the thought. "The Cleaner is finally clean. Thank you, Lord. Thank you, my Savior," Charlie whispers.

Charlie sloshes his mop into the water bucket. As he brings it out a little too enthusiastically, he places it on top of the new doctor's foot.

"I'm so sorry, Doctor. Please forgive me," says Charlie.

There's a tidal wave of panic starting to rise inside him.

But Dr. Michael smiles at Charlie. "No harm done. Don't give it another thought. I'm Dr. Michael. I've heard good things about you."

"You have?" Charlie asks. He can't hide his surprise.

Dr. Michael laughs. "Don't look so surprised. Everyone knows how hard you work. Even Brandon, the head of the Peacekeepers, says good things about you now. They all know that you've done wonders with Alphina."

Charlie doesn't know what to say or what to do so he just stands there holding his dripping mop in the air.

"Keep up the good work, Charlie," Dr. Michael says heartily. Then he leans in as he shakes Charlie's hand and whispers, "Merry Christmas. Keep the faith, my brother."

Ben and Heather

CHRISTMAS DAY

Both Ben and Heather smell the bread baking. They almost run into each other as they are trying to get to the kitchen. Both laugh at this near collision.

"I have something for you, Heather," Ben says.

"You do?"

"It's not much. Merry Christmas." He hands her a small envelope.

"Ben, I don't have a present for you," says Heather.

"That's okay. I didn't expect anything. This is something very small." Heather takes the envelope, looks inside, and immediately knows what it means. She pulls out a dried daisy. "Oh, Ben, thank you so much."

"The story from Alphie about The Little Daisy, I think she was talking about you. You bloom wherever you are. You're … you're beautiful."

Heather steps forward and takes Ben's hand. "I love you, too, Ben. Merry Christmas."

Ben takes a step closer to Heather and hugs her, knowing that the Lord has brought them together for such a time as this. Then he kneels on the floor on one knee. He takes Heather's hands in his. "Heather, I know that we haven't known each other very long. And yet I feel as if I know everything I need to know about you. You are kind and caring. Smart and talented. You always think of others before yourself. And you love the Lord.

"We don't know what tomorrow holds. We don't know how long either of us will live in this upside down, crazy world. We don't know if the Lord will come back today and take us home. But I do know that I would be indescribably honored if you would marry me. Will you marry me, Heather?"

Without hesitation, Heather answers, "Yes, Ben. I will gladly marry you. Merry Christmas!"

Ray and Molly

CHRISTMAS DAY

"Rise and shine, Ray! It's Christmas day!" says Molly.

"Merry Christmas, Love! I can already tell it's going to be a great day!" Ray is chipper this morning. He jumps out of bed and gives his wife a bear hug and a kiss. "I thank the Lord for you, Molly!"

"Oh, Ray. I thank Him for you, too. I always have and I always will!"

Just then they hear a faint knocking on the basement door. "Come down," says Molly.

Frank and Jonah sneak down the stairs with the fragrant greenery and ribbon in hand. "Oh, good!" says Molly. "You found some." They get busy and make one of the prettiest Christmas wreaths around. Well, the only one around, but it's still pretty.

"Mom is going to love this," says Jonah. "Thanks for your help, Miss Molly."

"You're so welcome, Jonah. That ribbon adds so much."

"Miss May let me have it. I found it in a closet. I wasn't snooping, just looking for hidden treasures. Miss May said that was okay. She says this house is full of hidden treasures and it's about time someone finds them and uses them."

"She's a wise woman," says Frank smiling.

Upstairs Beth and Erin find Pearl. "Is it time, yet?" they both ask excitedly.

"No, not quite. But it will be soon," answers Pearl. "Let's get everything organized though."

They go through their secret pile and make sure each item is wrapped in brown paper. They cut up brown paper sacks to make the wrapping. Earlier, the girls decorated the sacks with drawings and wrote each person's name on their sack. Now they place a sack by each place at the table.

"Thank you, Miss Pearl," says Beth.

Erin quickly chimes in. "Yes, thank you, Miss Pearl! Thanks for letting us help you."

"You girls did most of the work, I just guided you along."

"Do you think they'll like them?" asks Erin.

"How could they not like them?" asks Pearl. "Let's leave quickly now before anyone sees us."

The day passes quickly. Finally, it's time to sit down to dinner. All 12 of them sit together in the large dining room. The multiple loaves of bread fill up the table. Various jars of jam from the root cellar look inviting. Even though they've been there for many years, May and Frank tested the contents and found it was all still good.

In the middle of the table lies the beautiful wreath Jonah made for his mom. Daisy notices it immediately. "Oh, what a lovely wreath! It makes me think of Christmas."

"It's for you, Mom," says Jonah. "Frank and Miss Molly and Ray helped me with it. Miss May gave me the ribbon. Do you like it?"

"I love it, Jonah! Thank you. Thank you all. It reminds me of when we first came her. When Jonah and I stepped through the second grove of evergreen trees he said, "This place smells like Christmas.' There's a little bit of Christmas at our table."

Daisy sees all the brown paper wrapped gifts. "What are these?" she asks.

"These are from Erin, Miss Pearl, and me. Open them!" says Beth.

Each person opens a square piece of fabric. On each square is an appliqued heart. "How pretty!" says Heather.

"Yes!" agrees Molly. "They are beautiful."

"They're for a quilt. We can all help. Miss Pearl will show us how," says Erin.

"We tried to pick out colors of fabric we thought would fit each one of you. May let us use scraps she had in a closet. We're all so different and yet the Lord has brought us all together for such a time as this. We are being quilted together as a family."

"How perfect," Ben says as Ray the plumber wipes away tears.

"I'm just an old crybaby anymore. See what you people have done to me," says Ray. Everyone at the table laughs. Molly squeezes Ray hand.

"Ray, will you say grace for us tonight on this very special night?" asks May.

Ray begins, "Dear Heavenly Father, thank you for this group of people who are now my family. Thank you for sending Jesus to earth as a small baby. He is our special Christmas gift. Because of your love for us, we can now be forgiven for our sins. We love you. We praise you. We thank you. Merry Christmas! Amen."

After everyone has their fill of May's wonderful bread and homemade jam they're relaxing. Each one thinking about Christmas and the birth of their Savior. Each one content and for once, not worried about the outside world.

Even Daisy and Kate, who continue to pray faithfully for their husbands several times a day, are relaxed.

Suddenly, there's a loud, angry banging on the front door.

It sounds like it will break. May looks at Frank. Heather looks at Ben. Kate looks at Erin and Beth. Daisy looks at Jonah. Jonah looks at Pearl. Ray looks at Molly.

They see bright search lights. And they all hear the same sound. The sound of wood and glass breaking.

Dear Oliver

CHRISTMAS DAY EVENING

Dear Oliver,
This may be the last letter I write. Dr. Michael was arrested a little while ago. They found a Bible among his things. I guess the authorities routinely search employees' quarters, too. They don't trust anyone. Especially someone like Dr. Michael who's making a real difference around here. He's actually helping people, not just going through the motions.

I overhead some of them talking outside my door. In the front of his Bible, Dr. Michael wrote: "I dedicate my life to you, my Lord. Help me live courageously and selflessly just like my best friend Timothy did. He jumped in front of the school shooter to save my life. He knew I wasn't a believer. By sacrificing himself, he gave me another chance of life. But it was when I thought about what he'd told me about You, Lord, that my life was truly saved."

I'm not sure if Dr, Michael is being taken to re-education camp, the firing squad, or worse. They may be planning something horrific to televise. Remember the early days? The Roman arenas with the hungry lions? Those people look like amateurs compared to the ones in charge now.

Whatever happens to Dr. Michael, I thank the Lord that he was part of my life, if only for a short time. I'm praying for him. Please pray, too.

The authorities are now scrutinizing all his patients. They've already taken many to the room. You know which one. The one we only see people enter but never leave. I expect them to come for me any minute. It's okay. I'm at peace.

Until they do, though, I want you to know that the Lord is with us, dear Oliver. He always has been. He always will be. And I want you to know that this has been such a privilege for me to work together with you for the Lord's people for such a time as this. Don't worry about me. If I go home to the Lord, all the better. And He will bring someone else to take my place.

Keep the faith, my brother. Merry Christmas! Our Savior lives!

Love, Alphie

Alphie takes the paper out of her old Oliver typewriter and tapes it to the wall next to a few others. She turns around in time to see the head Peacekeeper, Brandon, at her door. He's not alone. He's armed with his gun in his hand and a scowl on his face. As he turns the doorknob Alphie whispers, "Lord, into thy hands I commend my spirit."

Kathy Yoder started writing when she was eight years old. A weekly faith columnist at Iowa's *Sioux City Journal* since December 2004 and a Religion Communicators Council Wilbur Award winner, Yoder has a master's degree in English, art, and mass communication, with an emphasis on creative writing. She's a former photojournalist, the former Director of Children's Ministries, retired healthcare chaplain, and licensed minister. Learn more at www.kathyyoder.com.

1

www.ingramcontent.com/pod-product-compliance
Lightning Source LLC
Chambersburg PA
CBHW060359030726
47497CB00003B/785